The Windmill

Also by Stephanie Gertler

Jimmy's Girl

The Puzzle Bark Tree

Drifting

The
Windmill

STEPHANIE GERTLER

DUTTON

DUTTON
Published by Penguin Group (USA) Inc.
375 Hudson Street, New York, New York 10014, U.S.A.
Penguin Group (Canada), 10 Alcorn Avenue, Toronto, Ontario, Canada M4V 3B2
(a division of Pearson Penguin Canada Inc.); Penguin Books Ltd, 80 Strand,
London WC2R 0RL, England; Penguin Ireland, 25 St Stephen's Green, Dublin 2,
Ireland (a division of Penguin Books Ltd); Penguin Group (Australia), 250
Camberwell Road, Camberwell, Victoria 3124, Australia (a division of Pearson
Australia Group Pty Ltd); Penguin Books India Pvt Ltd, 11 Community Centre,
Panchsheel Park, New Delhi – 110 017, India; Penguin Group (NZ), Cnr Airborne
and Rosedale Roads, Albany, Auckland, New Zealand (a division of Pearson
New Zealand Ltd); Penguin Books (South Africa) (Pty) Ltd, 24 Sturdee Avenue
Rosebank, Johannesburg 2196, South Africa
Penguin Books Ltd, Registered Offices: 80 Strand, London WC2R 0RL, England

Published by Dutton, a member of Penguin Group (USA) Inc.

First printing, November 2004
1 3 5 7 9 10 8 6 4 2

Ⓓ REGISTERED TRADEMARK—MARCA REGISTRADA

LIBRARY OF CONGRESS CATALOGING-IN-PUBLICATION DATA

Gertler, Stephanie.
The windmill / By Stephanie Gertler.
p. cm.
ISBN 0-525-94800-7 (alk. paper)
1. Women college teachers—Fiction. 2. Loss (Psychology)—Fiction. 3. Runaway
husbands—Fiction. 4. Remarried people—Fiction. 5. Missing persons—Fiction.
6. Massachusetts—Fiction. 7. Secrecy—Fiction. I. Title.
PS3557.E738W56 2004
813'.6—dc22   2004006709

Printed in the United States of America
Set in Palatino

PUBLISHER'S NOTE

This book is printed on acid-free paper. ∞

To my children
David, who never ceases to astound me
Ellie, who has the wisdom and beauty of an old soul
Ben, who has a perspective way beyond his years
I love you

Acknowledgments

Once again, there are many people to thank: Chip Crosby for his literary enthusiasm, psychological expertise, and Mozart's piano concerto number 23—the adagio that was an inspiration; John Staffieri for advice in law enforcement; Alysyn Balentine (my "imaginary friend") for her sweetness, courage, and the local color of North Carolina, past and present; Chip Smith for assistance in matters of changing identity; Judy Aronson for her wisdom, family, and a historic pictorial of Cape Cod; Cheryl Franks for explanations of racial conditions in the South in the 1960s; Frank Gertler for insight into the mind of a scientist; Tom Vris for remembrances of Greenwich Village way back when; Brian Donnell for reading the predictions in the Eight Ball.

Thanks also to Ronni Berger for always being there and to my agent, Stephanie Rostan, a great reader—here's to the start of something new! My gratitude to Carole Baron and Julie Doughty for editorial insights, patience, and assistance beyond belief.

And to all those I know and love: You know who you are. You know your names.

The Windmill

CHAPTER ONE

Olivia

I am still not exactly certain what compelled me to go to Carl's office that Friday morning last November. Looking back, I believe it was instinct or intuition. He was troubled at breakfast that morning, more deeply immersed in thought than usual—even for Carl. We sat with our mugs of coffee, read the newspaper, planned the weekend when we would rake the leaves and sweep away the last of autumn's debris from the gutters.

He pushed back his chair, carried his mug to the sink, and, when typically he would grab his overcoat from the rack by the door and call "See you later" as he walked out, he came over and kissed my cheek. "See you," he said, lingering for a moment.

"See you," I said in a puzzled echo.

It wasn't until later, once I knew he was gone, that the inherent finality in his voice resonated within me. Carl was saying good-bye.

I arrived early to teach my eleven o'clock class as I often do. Since Daniel and Sophie are away at school, morning chores are far less demanding. Usually, I go to the deli across the street from campus and have a second cup of coffee. I call my sister Nina or my parents from the cell phone but, instead, I went to Carl's office in the science building on the other side of campus. It is an older building, darkened stone and ivy-covered. The door is frosted glass in a dark wood frame; DEPARTMENT OF

PHYSICS stenciled in muddy brown. As I tried the knob, Ginny, Carl's secretary, pulled open the door.

"He's not here. Where is he?" she asked, almost as though I'd stolen him.

She startled me. "What are you talking about?"

"I didn't mean to alarm you, Ms. Hughes. But he's not here. Dr. Larkin. He's not here," she said breathlessly.

"I don't understand," I said, truly not getting the impact of what she said even though she kept repeating herself.

"Dr. Larkin didn't show up for work this morning," she said, enunciating each syllable as though we didn't speak the same language. "I thought maybe you'd know why."

I have mastered the art of transporting myself to another place in time when I feel cornered. Nina says it is the essence of protective animal instinct. And so I thought of garbage soup. I stood with my lips parted slightly and stared at Ginny, my mind back in the kitchen with my mother when Nina and I were girls. She was making a stew and Nina and I were dumping all the scrapings—potato peel, brown celery tips, the fat she'd trimmed off meat, chips of bone and gristle—into a giant pot of water. It was something you'd never want to look at, let alone taste. I suppose that Carl's absence was just like that crazy concoction.

Thoughts raced through my mind the way they do in a dream. Rapid, all jumbled together, and barely discernible. Part of me wondered if I had willed this to happen. Certainly there had been times when I wished Carl would just go away. No harm, no drama, no major scenes. I can't imagine there isn't a wife on Earth who hasn't felt that way at one time or another. Or a husband, for that matter. But Carl was far too practical to simply disappear, let alone deviate from his routine. That he was not where he was supposed to be was unsettling. It was the antithesis of Carl. My grandmother always said, "Be careful what you wish for."

Poor Ginny. She'd been there for nearly a year and had the

patience of a saint, unlike the string of temps who preceded her. There she was, her stringy brown hair tied back with a limp chiffon kerchief, her navy skirt dotted with lint, her eyes wide and clearly panic-stricken beneath thick-lensed glasses. She was probably in her mid-forties although she could have just as easily been sixty.

"Ms. Hughes? I'm looking to see if I missed something," Ginny said, scanning Carl's appointment book, running her index finger up and down the columns, flipping pages back and forth, as though she might find the Perfectly Reasonable Explanation as to why he wasn't there. She kept muttering, "I can't understand where he is," over and over again, the way we do when we misplace something.

"Now, let's just think for a moment," I said. "You've checked his book." As the words left my mouth, I realized how ridiculous they were. I was trying to calm her down—and myself—in the hope that this was all some sort of misunderstanding or miscommunication.

She looked at me blankly, down at the book in front of her, then back at me. "I *am* checking," she said.

"I'm sorry. I wasn't thinking," I said. "What time did you get here this morning? I mean, maybe he got here before you did and then left. He left the house at seven-thirty."

"I got here around seven-thirty," she said softly. "The bus was on time this morning."

"Well, maybe he had a dentist appointment or something."

We both knew I was grasping at straws.

"Actually, he went to the dentist *last* week," she said meekly.

"Right. I forgot," I mumbled, though truly I hadn't known.

"Well, there has to be some explanation," I said. "Something must have come up that he forgot to mention."

Ginny's mouth was so parched that there were sticky little white patches in the corners. "I suppose," she said. "It's just so unlike him."

Ginny inadvertently validated my fears. We both knew that Carl made no appointments by himself. His scheduling was precise and executed with constant reminders from whomever was assisting him that week or that month: Post-Its stuck on his computer and on top of his mail and then, finally, someone practically ushering him out the door with more last-minute re-minders telling him for the umpteenth time the name of the person he was meeting, the location—even the topic. Carl's poor secretaries did everything but slick down his hair, stick an identification tag on his lapel, and hang his car key around his neck. They booted up his computer, returned his phone mes-sages, retrieved his voice mail, his e-mail, and generally ran in-terference among his colleagues, who found Carl to be brilliant but distracted to the point of vacancy. Those who didn't know Carl well might have thought him to be condescending or aloof. It wasn't that at all. Carl was just profoundly introspective, private, and abysmally disorganized—the reasons why the temps usually threw their hands up in the air after a month or so and quit.

I played a game in my head sometimes: How would I an-swer if someone asked me to describe my husband? "Carl Larkin, fifty-eight years old. Chairman of the Department of Physics at Belvedere College in Willow, Massachusetts." Hand-some and rugged in a rumpled, absentminded professor sort of way. He lived and breathed physics, waxing on and on about his fascination with the "duality of pairs." He was a self-admitted loner, although I believed that, deep down inside, he cherished his children and even me. He presented himself as though he had an aversion to intimacy although I often won-dered whether it was avoidance or fear. He seemed to eschew metaphor, symbolism, or emotion and yet I often felt that was a disguise as well. Whenever I attempted to scratch beneath Carl's surface, a nearly visible armor covered him. At that very moment, I chastised myself for not being more relentless with

Carl, for retreating so easily instead of forcibly penetrating him. But, then again, had I reached into his soul, I would have had to allow him to reach into mine.

The week before Carl disappeared, I turned fifty. People say "It's just a number," but fifty is synonymous with words like "milestone" and "turning point." Epithets that do little to soften the blows from AARP cards coming in the mail and children who remind us that fifty is half a century. Certainly, it's an age that begs us to take stock. Once, a long time ago, I thought I would be an actress. When the kids entered grade school, I began teaching drama at Belvedere, a poor substitute for the stage but my life had changed: I was married with children. Another physics professor, a colleague of Carl's, once joked that I was undoubtedly Carl's id: Carl was matter and I was spirit. Carl was concrete where I was abstract. Diametric opposition, he said, but of course, they say that opposites attract. It was that sort of evaluation, that coming-of-age examination of myself and my marriage, that occupied me for the months before my birthday.

I took the appointment book from Ginny's desk and flipped through the pages. "People don't just disappear," I said, closing the book, placing it back on the desk, reassuring myself as much as I was reassuring her.

"I hope he's OK," she said softly.

"Carl can take care of himself," I said unconvincingly.

Ginny nodded—just as unconvincingly.

"Are you sure nothing odd happened in the last day or so?" I sounded more like a detective than a wife. "You're not forgetting something?"

"I don't think so, Ms. Hughes."

"Anything distressing about a grant he didn't get or something like that? That always eats him up inside."

Ginny paled. "You're not thinking he was in some sort of *state*?"

"No. Not at all. I'm thinking that maybe there's something he failed to mention or just mentioned casually. Maybe he had to meet with administration or something." I swallowed. "You know, like something last-minute."

She was pulling up Carl's e-mails now. I looked over her shoulder and could see it was mostly spam. "It's been a quiet week," she said.

"So, nothing?"

"Well, he met with a student on Monday who wanted to change his lab date." Ginny inhaled deeply. "But that happens all the time."

"What does?"

"Kids wanting to change labs and tests and whatever."

"And Carl usually handles that?"

"No, actually, he doesn't," she said. "Dr. Larkin just happened to be in the outside office and, since I was on a phone call to NIH, Dr. Larkin was good enough to take care of it."

"And?"

"And nothing. The boy changed his lab and that was that."

"Well, I tell you what. I'll keep you posted if I hear anything and you do the same." I smiled. "I'm sure by the end of the day, we'll have this all straightened out. Now if he calls you . . ."

"I'll have him get in touch with you right away, Ms. Hughes, not to worry."

I squeezed her hand. "Thanks, Ginny."

I made a loop around the campus just to see if Carl's car was parked outside one of the other buildings. I even drove by the dorms, though I knew that Carl had to be smarter than to park his car by a dorm if he was having an affair with a coed. I went to the Shell station hoping his car was there with a flat, or that his car was due for inspection or something. I drove back to campus and was late for my class. I checked in with Ginny before rehearsal for *Antigone* later that afternoon.

"Ms. Hughes, you don't think you should call . . ."

"The police?" I asked, my heart pounding. "I'm not sure."

"Is there anything else I can do?"

I looked at my watch. "It's almost five, Ginny. Why don't you just go home?"

⑨

It was nearly seven when I left the auditorium. I checked my cell phone even though I'd left it turned on throughout rehearsal. There were no messages. Last fall was unseasonably warm until mid-November. The leaves never turned the way they usually did—just fell lifeless to the ground. As I walked to my car, the combination of pitch black and balmy warmth was particularly disorienting. There was a scent of smoke and dust in the air. I'd mentioned it to Carl just the evening before when we were walking Emmet, our half-Lab, half-Shepherd.

"What is that smell?" I asked.

"Mold," he said, matter-of-factly.

"Mold? Can you *smell* mold? Really?"

"When it's bad enough."

I shrugged. "That's it?"

"Mold and mildew," he said. He smiled at me. "What did you think?"

"I was hoping for something more romantic. Shooting stars heating up the earth."

"Shooting stars are just temporary. They're really just rocks that catch fire. They don't scorch the earth."

You see? Duality of pairs.

Even though Carl's car wasn't in the driveway, I called his name as I walked in the door. I was enveloped with emptiness when there was no answer. I thought of Sophie and Daniel and how I would explain that their father was missing.

I was hanging up my coat when I caught my image in the oval mirror that hangs above the boot bench in our vestibule. For a moment someone else was there. Surely, it wasn't my reflection. Mine would be someone younger, with a defined jaw and wide eyes. A sense of time and dread came over me like webbing.

I heard the faint drone of the old boiler and the hollow clicks of my heels on the ceramic floor. Our ramshackle house on the Connecticut River suddenly felt unfamiliar. It appeared dilapidated, accusing me of neglect: The carpets were shiny with age and sprinkled with paint chips. There were piles of papers in places where papers didn't belong—on the dining table and the kitchen counter. Old newspapers, unopened mail. Junk. Too much junk lying around. Emmet nuzzled my leg. He'd been sleeping in his spot under the kitchen table.

"Some watchdog you are, " I said, stroking his head. "So, tell me, where is he?"

I opened and closed the refrigerator. The thought of food was unappealing although my stomach growled. I hadn't eaten since breakfast. I walked up the stairs and opened doors to every room, slowly, carefully, afraid of what I might find—Carl crumpled on a floor, beyond resuscitation—something horrific like that. Finding nothing was a relief.

It seemed rather premature, but I called the police. My hands shook as I dialed.

"Willow Police."

"My husband didn't show up for work this morning," I said. "He's missing."

"Hang on," the person sang as though I called for a hair appointment.

I was patched through to the detective division where Detective Rossi listened as I explained that Carl never got to work that morning. The detective punctuated his attention with "uh-huh" every few seconds.

"So, why do you want to report him missing if he just didn't show up for work?"

"Because he *always* shows up for work."

"We don't take reports on competent adults with no medical or mental history for forty-eight hours," he said. "He doesn't have one, right?"

"Right."

"What's his license plate?"

I told him and he left the line for a moment. "We have no reports on the car."

"What does that mean?"

"No accidents. Not stolen."

"I see."

"Ma'am, are you having marital problems?"

"No. Well, I mean, every marriage has something," I said defensively.

And then he just went on. Do you think he's having an affair? Does he have a drinking problem? Did you argue before he left? Did he leave at the same time that morning? Did he wear the clothes that morning that he usually wears? How was his demeanor last night? Has he ever disappeared like this before? Any enemies? Friends I could call and who might know where he'd gone. What about his cell phone?

When I said that Carl didn't own a cell phone, that surprised the detective more than Carl's disappearance.

"Call Sunday if he's not back by then," he said as though I'd merely lost my wallet.

"Sunday? But he's my husband."

"That's protocol, ma'am. Sorry."

I was about to hang up when he said, "Oh, and you might want to check the twenty-four-hour line at the bank."

"What for?"

"Cash withdrawals," he said bluntly.

"I don't understand."

"Sometimes, if someone is planning to leave for a while, they'll take cash with them."

Clearly Detective Rossi had been down this road before, and

I wondered how many wives called for the same reason. I called the bank and nothing had been withdrawn from either checking or savings. Part of me thought I might have felt better had he emptied an account. At least then I would have known this was calculated, that he was alive and had simply left me. Emmet nuzzled me again. I patted his head but he kept pulling at my hand. In all the commotion, I'd forgotten to feed him.

We keep a thirty-pound bag of food in a covered barrel in the mud room. I grabbed Emmet's bowl and there, taped to the side of the barrel, was a blue envelope with the Belvedere insignia.

Dear Livi,
Forgive me. I have started this letter a half dozen times and conclude that the only thing I can tell you right now is that I am fine. I haven't lost my mind and intend no harm to come to myself. I will explain. I promise. I'll call by Monday. I do love you.
Carl

I read the letter over and over, trying to read between the few scrawled lines, astonished and frightened because Carl said he loved me. When was the last time we'd told each other? I couldn't remember. I folded the letter into my pocket and grabbed my coat. I needed to go down to the river. Emmet abandoned his food and followed me. I used to take Daniel and Sophie to the river when they were little. We'd pack a picnic basket and bring piles of picture books and Old Maid cards and sit on the weathered dock until the sun set over the old footbridge that crossed the narrows.

Another wife might have waited by the telephone or sat and wrung her hands that night. She might have called friends for comfort and conversation, vacillating between worry and anger, rationalization and fear. Honestly, except for Nina and my parents, there was no one to call. I was as much a loner as Carl. Instead, Carl's absence lured me to a place I'd resisted and needed to think about—back to the summer of 1978 when it was I who disappeared, only to return a few years later as Carl Larkin's wife.

CHAPTER TWO

Olivia

In 1978, my mother was only five years older than I am today. She is eighty now, and still the most beautiful creature I have ever seen. Even her skin remains strangely smooth and supple. Back then, she wore narrow black pedal pushers and a crisp white shirt, her thick dark hair tied back in a bright kerchief. Now, she wears baby-blue or blush-pink housecoats and her hair falls in thin silver wisps around her face. The sparkle has left her blue eyes. My father is seven years older than my mother. Until just a year or so ago, he knew my name. Now he calls me Nina sometimes, and sometimes he calls my sister Olivia. He also calls me Evelyn, his older sister who died when they were children. But he never forgets my mother's name. "Margaret! Meg!" he frequently calls for no discernible reason yet my mother runs toward the sound of his voice each time. He needs to know that she's still there. All she wants is to be there beside him.

My parents, Henry and Margaret Hughes, still live in the simple putty-colored house on the beach in Chatham where I grew up in Cape Cod, Massachusetts. It has a single brick chimney and a slate path set in equal squares leading to a door nestled under a small covered porch. It is the house where my father grew up with four brothers and two sisters. It is filled with memories carved into wood floors and etched on windowpanes in the form of initials, names, and dates—reminding us who was once there.

Throughout his life, my father swore that Cape Cod was the best place to live. The only place to live. He wouldn't, as we say on the Cape, go over the bridge. He'd been to Europe once, during the War, and swore he'd never cross the sea again for "good reason" and never did. He flew the flag on our front porch from Memorial Day through Labor Day and would have flown it right into winter if not for the snow and ice that could cause damage.

My mother always wanted to go to Italy. She's never been abroad or anywhere north of Quebec, west of Amherst, or south of Washington, D.C. Last year, after Daniel went off to college, Nina and my mother and I planned a ten-day trip to Italy— we'd fly into Florence and drive the Amalfi coast—but then my father's mind began to fail and she wouldn't leave him. Nina and I believed that even if he had been strong and clear, she would have found a last-minute excuse not to go. In their fifty-eight years together, they'd never been apart for more than a few days and that was when she gave birth to us. Nina and I went to Florence and Venice, and brought back Venetian glass and silk scarves for our mother. She opened the boxes and squealed like a child at Christmas, winding all the beaded strands around her neck at once and layering the scarves on top of them. "You'd think I was the one who was getting daft!" she said, laughing. Getting daft: My father was further gone than daft but my mother clung to hope.

One summer morning in 1978, my mother went into town and bought a small tub of rouge at the pharmacy, an enormous departure for this woman whose only cosmetic was the salt air. It was way too red for her complexion, painting her with a tubercular look that did little to cover the pallor which drained the rose of her cheeks. I had taken a toll on her that summer.

She didn't leave my side, barely slept, and didn't walk the beach or tend the garden with my father as she usually did in summer. Looking back, I now know it wasn't only *my* life that changed that summer. She tiptoed into my room each night, gripping the doorknob tightly, turning it slowly so I wouldn't be awakened by the catch, much the same way she did when Nina was an infant and I watched while her palm lay on Nina's back, feeling her breathe. The same way Nina and I did with our babies. My mother studied me that summer. Was I that fragile? I was certain she thought I might die of a broken heart. What other reason was there to watch me sleep? I always heard the catch and then the creak of the old door but I pretended to be sleeping. That was what she wanted. Besides, pretending was my strong suit that summer, and perhaps since then as well.

One afternoon, my mother carried a painted tray with a pitcher of amber iced tea circled by four cranberry-colored glass mugs into the sun room where I sat each day for nearly two months. She set down the tray on the baby grand piano and came to me, placing her cool lips on my forehead and the back of her hand against my cheek as she had when I was a little girl and had a fever. When she was young, my mother was a registered nurse. She had a way about her that was calm and easy and confident whenever Nina and I were sick. But her lips to my forehead was just another helpless gesture that summer. I suppose she hoped my lethargy was merely the result of a fever or some physical but mild illness that could be explained and cured with a Bufferin. If only my immobilizing pain was something other than despair that kept me motionless on the cushioned seat below the beveled window that looked over Nantucket Sound. My old thinking place. I called it My Escape on the Cape. When I was a teenager, I drew the lined floral chintz draperies around me, lost in dreamy late-night thoughts that read like poetry. The only light came from the rhythmic blinking of the beacon from the Chatham Lighthouse and, on clear nights, the moon. That summer, each time I drew the draperies around me, longing to burrow into a cocoon, someone tore them open with a jarring pull of the string or frantic struggle to separate them at the middle and then, with visible relief, they asked if I was OK, their breath still caught in their throats when they saw I was upright. The phone rang continually—neighbors and friends and relatives—calling to ask "How's Livi today?" as though by some miracle I might have healed overnight.

My mother filled the mugs, talking half to herself and half to me. I ignored her, leaning back against the wall, the draperies caught behind me, the fabric straining precariously from the cornice overhead. I sat with my knees bent, my hands limply on my thighs. A flowing yellow batik skirt grazed the arch of my bare feet, a beige crocheted shawl that had been my grandmother's covered my shoulders.

"You're going to pull down that cornice if you lean against it like that," my mother cautioned.

I didn't answer.

"Careful, Livi. Move the fabric."

I leaned forward so the draperies fell away from me.

"So hot today, Livi," my mother said, forcing a lilt to her voice. "Your father's been watering the garden all morning. It's just drinking it up. We could use some rain. I can't recall a drier summer."

My father's heavier footsteps came into the hall. His gardening shoes dropped to the floor. He came into the sun porch and, from the corner of my eye, I saw his head cock in my direction as he looked at my mother, who responded with a not-subtle-enough negative shake of hers. My father placed his rough hand on my shoulder, a gesture filled with a thousand words of comfort. I pressed my cheek into his hand that smelled faintly of roses and damp earth. His tenderness made everything feel

worse since my father was, typically, gruff and resisted sentiment. A cry welled in my throat as he cupped my cheek in his
palm and I felt that my bones might dissolve and turn to dust.
Just then, Nina came in, her bell-bottom jeans trailing along the
floor, a broad multicolored cloth belt hanging down one side,
her peasant blouse slipping off her suntanned shoulder. Nina
was my guardian angel that summer. She positioned herself on
the window seat opposite me, kicked off her sandals, and placed
her bare feet on top of mine.

"How come your feet are so cold?" she asked, squiggling her
toes against mine. "Here, I'll warm them up."

"Look at the strings on those denims, Nina," my father said.
"People will think I can't afford to buy you decent clothes."

"It's really not attractive, Nina," my mother said. "I could
hem them, you know. Or at least let me trim them with the
pinking shears. You look like a street urchin."

Nina sighed. "They're not denims. They're blue jeans and I
like them this way. They're called Landlubbers and they cost
twenty dollars. Street urchins can't afford Landlubbers."

On one hand, I wanted my family to go away, to silence
them. On the other, their banter and vain attempts to cajole me
made me feel alive.

"Today is one month," I said. My voice sounded guttural
and remote.

"We know," Nina said, her eyes wide as she stared at me, her
mouth forming the words as one might speak to someone who
reads lips.

I leaned forward and placed my hands between my knees.
"You can't all keep up the vigil, you know. I'm not in a coma.
It's like you're waiting for me to come to. I don't know what
you want from me."

"Now, now," my mother said, pouring an iced tea and handing it to my father. "Enough of that talk. Here, Henry."

"You steep this in the sun, Margaret?" my father asked after taking a sip. "I tell you this isn't tea. This is nectar, Olivia. Sweet, sweet nectar."

My father always said that whenever my mother handed him a glass of iced tea filled with fresh lemon juice that she squeezed in the ceramic hand press.

"You say the same thing every time," I said, massaging the back of my neck and shutting my eyes. When I looked up, their gazes were fixed on me. "What?"

"Well, it is like nectar," my father said defensively, picking up where we'd left off.

"I'll take one, Mommy," I said.

Her face brightened. "Now you see? This isn't a vigil," she said. "Livi, I thought maybe you and Nina and I could drive up to Provincetown this evening. There's a new little café and a street art show. Brass bas-relief sculpture. Or we can see what's showing at the Dennis Playhouse. Your father's got a VFW meeting tonight so he won't miss us. Right, Henry? Veterans tonight, isn't it?"

Did she think if she kept talking, everything might feel right?

"I don't think so," I said. "You and Nina can go though. I'll be fine."

"I don't think you should stay alone . . . " my mother said, a look of alarm on her face.

Nina touched my arm. "Come on, Livi. Try. Come. You can't just sit here all the time."

Nina was twenty that summer, five years younger than I. My mother tried for eight years to conceive me and finally succeeded at the age of thirty. Nina was the surprise. We were both lean, muscular girls with long straight brown hair parted in the center. Large brown eyes fringed with thick lashes, straight noses, and heart-shaped lips. People always asked if we were twins. Now, people (rude people, Nina says, laughing) ask who's older. Since I turned fifty, I think it annoys Nina.

Nina took a deep breath. "Noah would want you to go tonight, Livi. He would."

"Nina!" my mother admonished. "Really!"

No one had mentioned Noah's name in weeks.

"It's OK, Mommy," I said. Did she think it hurt more to hear his name?

"I'm sorry, Livi," Nina said quietly. "Sorry."

I looked at her face. She loved him, too. Had I forgotten? She was only fourteen when they met and had an instant crush on him. He always played "Little Sister" when she was around and made her blush when he lip-synced the song to her.

I set the iced tea on the floor beside me. I tried to keep my voice even but it broke despite my effort. My breath came out in short spurts through my nose as I spoke. "He would want me to go. I just don't know if I can."

"Just for a little while," Nina whispered. "Try."

"I don't want to." I shut my eyes. I pictured his face. His carved fine-boned features. Wavy dark hair that was flecked with gold in the summer. The way he smiled at me and his eyes nearly danced. I pictured him shirtless, standing at our kitchen counter, reading the back of a cereal box while he waited for his toast to pop. His taut stomach with the thin trail of hair that went to his navel. I knew every inch of his body.

"An actor?" my father growled when I first told him about Noah. "I knew if you went to that drama school in New York you'd end up with some actor. Jesus, Mary, and Joseph, Olivia, you know what actors are like. Every damn one of them ends up waiting tables, and if they make a success of themselves they leave their wives and kids in the lurch and father kids out of wedlock and . . ."

I laughed. "He's different, Daddy. You'll see. He's perfect."

Then my father muttered something about no man being perfect and that damn Rudolph Valentino and stormed into his study.

But Noah *was* different. Noah and I spent our first weekend in Chatham six months after we'd met and about three months after we started not-so-secretly living together in the apartment on West Fourth Street. I was three weeks shy of nineteen and he was twenty-two.

That weekend Noah helped my father hang two particularly stubborn accordion doors and sand the deck. Even my father couldn't hide the fact that he was impressed. Noah stood behind my mother as she stirred fish chowder, his hand on her back as he peered into the pot and asked for a taste as a son would, not just a daughter's boyfriend. He and Nina shot hoops in the driveway and he taught her to dribble the ball behind her back. And then, after dinner that night, he walked into my father's study. God, he was so bold. My father was reading the evening paper and Noah said, "I'm in love with your daughter, Mr. Hughes."

I was peeking through the crack of the door.

My father set the newspaper on his lap. "Is she in love with you, too?"

Noah smiled. "She is. But I want you to know that I'll always make her happy, Mr. Hughes," Noah said. "I promise. You have my word."

How could someone with so ardent a promise have allowed what happened?

I first met Noah in the corridor of New York College's main building. I never walked in those days. I ran. Everything I did was at lightning speed, a result, I think, of the military way in which my father issued commands. He'd call me to help with something and then he'd punctuate the sentence with "Hurry up, Olivia!" I'd run to please him only to have him chastise me for rushing. So, there I was juggling books on top of an open bottle of Coca-Cola, holding a half-eaten donut from a white wax bag and, as I rounded a corner full-speed, there was Noah. He was moving in long deliberate strides, but I couldn't put on the brakes in time. We collided, the soda splashing into the air like a geyser and drenching him.

"Whoa! You always take the corners that fast? What did you do? Rob a bank?" He looked down at his soaked shirt and shook droplets of soda from a clipboard which held what appeared to be a script.

I recognized him from my Bergman class. He had one of those faces that reeked of movie star. "No. I mean, yes. Sorry. I am so sorry. Oh, God, look what I did to you."

I was mortified.

He pulled the wet T-shirt from his chest and handed me the clipboard. "Could you just take this for a moment, please?"

I fumbled with my books, trying to find a place to set them down before they tumbled so I could take the clipboard.

"Never mind," he said, a smile curling on his lips as he set the clipboard on the floor and wiped his hands on his jeans.

"I have tissues," I said digging into my jacket pocket. "Somewhere. Oh wait, better, I have napkins in the bag here . . . Oh God, they're sopped. I'm *so* sorry."

"*Sopped?* It's OK," he said, trying not to laugh. "I'll dry."

"I feel awful."

"I'm Noah. You?"

I stared at him. "I'm sorry," I said again.

He laughed. "That's your name?"

"What?"

"What's your name? I mean, don't you think we should know each other's names at this point? We've had a rather intimate encounter."

"Olivia," I said. "Livi."

"Livi. I like that. Listen. It's OK. I was surprised. That's all." I felt him looking at me but my eyes were down. "Hey, aren't you in the Bergman class?"

He'd noticed me. I nodded. "Yeah."

"Drama major, or are you just taking it for fun when you're not running track?"

"Drama major," I said, missing the joke.

He placed his hand on my shoulder. "Honest. It's OK." He looked at the clock as the bell rang. "So, I'll see you in class later, right?"

"Right," I said, my cheeks getting hotter by the minute and feeling less than brilliant.

Ugh. Could I have been any more tongue-tied? I felt like a total idiot, standing frozen, staring at his wet shirt as it molded to his chest and shoulders.

He waited for me after class that afternoon. I hadn't seen him in the lecture hall but there were more than two hundred people in the room and I was afraid to look.

"You changed your shirt," I said, thinking how good he looked dry.

"Yeah, seemed like a good idea," he said with a laugh. "Listen, you want to get a beer?"

"I can't. I'm supposed to meet with the TA for this course."

Noah shook his head. "Emerson? A real bastard. I hear."

"I never heard that."

"Oh, yeah. Clear case of a guy abusing his power. I take it you never met him? "

I shook my head no.

"Try not to stare at the wart on his nose."

"Wart?"

"It's this big thing that kind of hangs off the side . . . "

"I heard he was . . . " I didn't finish my sentence.

"You heard he was what?"

"I don't know. Nice looking, I guess." I blushed.

"You're joking? Emerson?"

"Oh, well, there's not much I can do now. I have a two o'clock appointment and I don't want to be late. He said I have twenty minutes. I'm not clear on Bergman. He's so, well, you know, esoteric." Good word, I thought. Maybe he wouldn't think I was such a dunce.

"Well, how about if I meet you outside his office around two-twenty then?"

"You?"

"Yeah, me."

"I don't know if we'll be done by then."

"Oh, you'll be done."

"How do you know?"

"When Emerson says twenty minutes, he means twenty minutes. And don't be late either. The guy's a time freak. He'll deduct points for tardiness."

"Come on. No one's that bad."

Noah shrugged. "It's your hanging. See you later."

I knocked on Emerson's door just moments after two o'clock.

"Come in," a deep voice boomed. "You're late, Miss Hughes."

The office was empty when I opened the door. "Mr. Emerson?" I called. My knees shook. What appeared to be a closet door was open. Suddenly, it slammed shut and a man came from behind. He wore a blue slicker, the hood tied beneath his chin.

"Noah Emerson, at your service."

"You? You're Mr. Emerson? I thought you had to be a grad student. Oh, God." I wanted to sink through the floor. "What is this? Payback for the soda incident?"

"To answer your first question, Miss Hughes, a TA can be either a grad student or an academically gifted senior." He bowed. "As for what you have so aptly termed the soda incident, Miss Hughes, you don't have any sort of liquid refreshment with you, do you? But, as you can see, I am totally prepared." He popped open an orange umbrella that was leaning inside the closet door.

"You're crazy! Where did you get all that stuff?"

"Props department. Sixth-floor theater."

"Close the umbrella! It's bad luck indoors." I couldn't stop laughing.

"I don't believe in bad luck, Miss Hughes." Noah closed the umbrella, pulled the slicker over his head and pushed the hair back from his forehead. "Now what's the problem with Bergman? Too deep? Too dark? Too *dry*, if you will? You don't like *dry* from what I've witnessed, do you, Miss Hughes?"

I couldn't stop laughing. "Maybe we should just go for that beer."

Noah smiled. "I'm really here to help you. They actually pay me to do this."

"I can't think straight. I don't even remember what I wanted to ask."

"Well, maybe it'll come to you over the beer."

"This was a dirty trick, you know."

"I couldn't resist." He smiled. "I'll buy the beers."

He opened the office door and placed his hand on my back as we walked out together. It took months for me to admit that it was my best friend Millie who encouraged me to meet the TA for the Bergman course. I understood Bergman just fine but Millie said that "Emerson" was rumored to be the cutest TA on campus.

Noah and I were inseparable from that moment on. Six months later we rented the tiny apartment on West Fourth. The whole place could have fit into my parents' living room, but it was amazing. It even had a rooftop garden. Actually, it was just a five-by-ten tarred flat roof where the previous tenant had left a rotted-out planter filled with cigarette butts and empty pints of Southern Comfort. We painted the tarred surface a deep green and Noah built a new planter where we planted basil and thyme and chives and marigolds. We bought two red canvas sling chairs at Azuma on Eighth Street and rescued a battered table someone had tossed on the curb and painted it with a red and white checkerboard pattern. In winter, we brought the table and chairs inside, slid them under our bed, and put the planter in the kitchen by the window. That first winter together after we brought the "roof" inside, we painted a mural of a sunrise behind our bed. We made our own world.

We married right after I graduated, with my father's blessing, although he never liked the idea that we lived in New York City. Finally, he resigned himself to what he called our need to get it out of our system—"it" being the city.

"One day you'll come to your senses and move out to the Cape," he said. "Why in God's name would anyone live on some claustrophobic cement island when you can live at the tip of the ocean? No wonder the place cost twenty-four dollars. You get what you pay for."

During the day Noah and I auditioned for plays—on Broadway, off-Broadway, in theaters with makeshift stages, and theaters that were there one day and gone the next. And at the end of every day, before our night shifts began at the restaurant where we eked out a living, we showered together and washed away stage make-up and all the sweat and soot that seemed to cling to us as we raced around Manhattan, and then we'd make love.

The summer of '78 was the first time we talked about leaving Manhattan. It wasn't the city we had known even just a few years before when Washington Square Park was filled with "peaceniks," as my father called them, strumming guitars and handing out anti-war leaflets. The boutiques and restaurants and mom-and-pop shops were closing down and giving way to chains like Nedick's and Whelan's and fast food places like Nathan's and Zum Zum. A lot of the little pubs we'd gone to in college were shutting down. Drug addicts and street people, derelicts for lack of a better description, drove the "peaceniks" from the park and wandered the streets and huddled in doorways. Even our apartment building was littered with empty liquor bottles and needles, and painted with obscene graffiti.

We had a long talk the Sunday night before it happened. We were sipping Mateus on the rooftop before we went to work.

"Sometimes I think we should just chuck it all and move out by your folks on the Cape," Noah said. "Open an acting studio or something. I always loved the city but it's not feeling so good anymore. It's changing. Not to mention that auditions aren't going so great."

It was a lot to say for someone like Noah who was a dyed-in-the-wool New Yorker. Brooklyn boy through and through.

"You're serious?" I asked.

He nodded. "I want to have a ton of kids. I want my ark, you know?" He grinned. "Two by two . . . "

"A ton of kids?" I leaned against him. "How many?"

He shrugged. "Eight. Twelve. And twin girls. I definitely want twin girls."

"Why twin girls?"

"Two more of you," he said, pulling me closer to him. "Two more skinny little brown-haired girls who walk too fast and gesture wildly with their hands and have heart-shaped lips and big brown eyes. Morgan and Tyler."

"Those sound like boys' names. Or a law firm." I laughed. "Besides, girls usually look like the father."

He shook his head. "Nope. Not these girls. I have it all planned."

"You do, do you?" I kissed his cheek.

"But we can't raise kids in the city. Not anymore." He sighed.

"You know Jeannie from the flower shop across the street? Her bike was stolen yesterday. She always chains it to the meter and someone cut right through the chain. It was broad daylight."

"So we should give this some thought," he said. "Serious thought. I'm not saying to do this right away. A year, maybe. Maybe two. I mean, if we had to, we could live with your folks for a while, right? We have options, right?"

Options. Noah loved options and visions and dreaming. Nothing was ever carved in stone for Noah. Nothing except for the two of us. Noah had the uncanny ability to take the most dire situation and spin it until it became serendipity, with either a lesson learned or a reason attached to it. When he didn't get a role he'd auditioned for, he said it was for the best since a better role would come along. He said that his view of life was validated the day we met. If I hadn't come flying around the bend with a bottle of Coca-Cola, I would have just been another girl in the Bergman class. Instead we got to look into each other's eyes and from that moment on he knew. It was preordained, he said. A chance meeting that wasn't really a chance.

While I sat on the window sill that summer, I wondered what he would have said of that night in July. Would he have said that was preordained, too? How would Noah have spun that?

We went to work after our talk and, as always, the restaurant was jammed. The bar was three deep and people waited in a line that stretched to the street. But tips would be good that night and the next day was Monday, when the restaurant was closed. Monday was our favorite day. I'd stop at Jefferson Market after auditions and buy the same thing each time: French bread, a wedge of cheese (Brie or Camembert, and to this day I can eat neither), a half pound of chuck, one onion, one green pepper, a can of tomato sauce, a can of tomato paste, and a bag of spaghetti. Noah usually brought home a bottle of wine. Mondays meant we'd have dinner together at our kitchen table with candles, or up on the roof if the weather was good, instead of standing at the end of the bar in the restaurant wolfing down whatever the manager said we could eat that night. Noah got home first on Mondays since I stopped at the market. He'd be waiting on the sofa in a pair of soft jeans and, depending on the season, either his favorite baggy cable-knit gray sweater or a worn T-shirt. Sometimes he'd be strumming his guitar, a cold beer on the table and another waiting for me in the fridge. When I got home that Monday, Noah wasn't there.

I was washing my face when I heard his key in the door.

"Where were you?" I called from the bathroom as I dried my face.

"Come here!" he called back.

I walked into the living room, the face cloth still in my hand.

"You're all pink!" he said. He handed me a single white rose, picked me up in the air and twirled me around. "I got it! I got the part! In this play called *Da*! Can you believe it?"

I jumped up and straddled his hips with my legs. "Oh my God! When did you hear?"

"I stopped at Elaine's on the way home. Don't even ask me why. I mean I wasn't planning to. I was at this audition today for a toothpaste commercial—that I didn't get, by the way, so we're no longer buying Pepsodent—in some hell hole of a building on West Fifty-Seventh Street by the river and when I was walking to the subway I thought I'd just stop up at Elaine's and see if she'd gotten us anything." He took a breath. "Anyway, I walk in the door and she says she was just about to call me. She says 'you must have ESP or something because the producer just called and you got the part.' Rehearsal starts next week. Two hundred a week, Livi. I'm buying champagne!"

"Champagne!" I said, laughing with tears in my eyes. "Noah, this is so wonderful. I am so proud of you."

"You're next, baby. Your turn is coming. I can feel it."

God, I loved when he called me baby. "We'll see. Listen, I'm starving. I'm going to start dinner."

"No, first we're going to have champagne." Noah was adamant. "We're celebrating."

"Well, ginger ale, maybe. I have two dollars in my purse."

"Raid the cookie jar, woman!"

"That's for emergencies."

"This is an emergency. How much do we have?"

"Twenty-three dollars and seventeen cents."

"What's with the seventeen cents?"

"I started saving pennies."

"No more pennies for us." He dragged me by the hand to the bedroom.

"What are you doing?"

He spoke in a French accent. "First I make love to zee wife. Then zee champagne."

"I thought it was the other way around. I thought you're supposed to get me drunk first."

"Nah, why waste good champagne? You've always been easy."

"Oh yeah? Easy for you," I said, blushing.

"Easy for me," he said softly kissing my face. "Do you know how much I love you, Mrs. Emerson?"

"I love you more," I said.

That was our only argument: who loved who more.

"Impossible," he said seriously. "It's just not possible."

We fell asleep afterward, tangled in one another while the sun set and the night became more humid. We walked up to the roof in our robes.

"It's going to storm," Noah said as a clap of thunder rolled. "I should go before it rains."

"We don't need champagne. We already celebrated."

He smiled. "I know. But we should have champagne. You know how your dad always pulls out champagne on special occasions."

"Wait 'til I tell Henry you're emulating him," I teased.

"The liquor store over on Sixth is open until nine."

"Why that one? We always go to Viola's."

"Viola's is closed. It's after seven."

"It's far," I pouted.

"It's a block away."

"I'm starving."

"Have something to hold you."

I laughed. "Something to hold me? Where did that come from?"

"Sorry I was temporarily possessed by an old woman." He laughed. "My grandmother used to say that. Listen, start cooking. I'll be back in a blink."

He gathered my hair in his hands and let it slip through his fingers onto my shoulders. I put my arms around his waist and leaned against his chest. "You're sure you'll still want all those kids? Will success spoil Noah Emerson?"

He wrapped his arms beneath my robe and caressed my bare back. "You know it's funny. This is all so great but I still keep thinking about that little place on the Cape." He took a deep breath. "I can't explain it. I'm happy about the part and this is something I need to do, but this isn't 'it,' you know what I mean? Does that sound make any sense?"

"It?"

"Yeah, you know, *it.* There's just more to life than . . . I just feel there's more, that's all."

I nodded. "Well, we have time to do both, right?"

"Right."

"I'm going to watch you in that show every night, you know."

He kissed my mouth and I will never forget that kiss. He murmured "I love you," and I murmured back to him and then I said, "Go. Before it begins to pour. The sooner you go, the sooner you'll come home."

We walked down the few stairs into the apartment. He stopped at the landing to take my hand as I stepped down. He pulled on his jeans and T-shirt. The rain was coming down in buckets when he left. He slipped into the sandals he left by the door and I told him that his feet would get soaked. I handed him the umbrella from the painted coffee can that we kept on the landing. He kissed my neck and he was gone.

I was cutting the baguette into narrow slices when I heard the sirens below the kitchen window. They got louder and stopped nearby with short staccato beats. Cars honked and wheels screeched and diesel fumes wafted through the open window. A fire engine clanged and wailed and came to a stop. A man called through a bullhorn to clear the area. I washed out two wineglasses, thinking that Noah should be back any moment, but my hands were shaking. I looked at the clock again. The minute hand was no longer moving.

🌀

I believe in different kinds of magic. The kinds of magic that made me collide with Noah in the hallway that day and the kind that stops a clock because something is wrong. Like a somnambulist making my way by sheer instinct, I dried my hands on a kitchen towel, took the house keys from my purse, and walked down the four flights to the street. There were flashing red lights on Sixth Avenue. The block away where the liquor store was. He was probably standing there in the crowd and watching, I thought, my heart pounding, my mouth so dry I couldn't swallow. Another poor bum scraped off the sidewalk, I told myself. Another stoned street person staggering into the intersection. I walked straight ahead and pushed my way through the human chain that lined the street, not caring that people were pushing me back. I heard someone say that the liquor store had been held up. A man was shot. I began to scream Noah's name. I *moaned* his name. It came from a place deep inside me where I never want to go again. A police officer approached, placed his hand on my shoulders and squared himself in front of me.

"Whose name are you calling, miss?" he asked.

"My husband," I sobbed. "Noah. Noah Emerson. My husband." My knees began to buckle.

I knew.

The police officer was solemn as he pulled me through the crowd. The ambulance was just leaving. He sat me down in the back of the patrol car with another officer. "He was in the wrong place at the wrong time," the officer said as I wept.

But Noah said there were reasons for everything, I thought. No. Something was wrong. This was all wrong. There was no reason for this.

I waited in the hallway of St. Vincent's Hospital in a stiff metal chair while Noah was in surgery, the scent of him still on my hands; the taste of him still in my mouth; my blouse stained with his blood. The nurses had let me lean over him and kiss him before they took him to the operating room. They must have known. Someone asked whom they could call for me and I gave them Millie's number. I didn't have the heart to call my parents or Nina. Besides, they were all too far away. Millie appeared just moments before the surgeon appeared an hour later.

"We tried," she said. "I'm so sorry."

The next thing I remember is morning. I can't remember going back to the apartment but, when I awakened, Millie was sitting beside me on the bed, holding my hand. I knew something horrible had happened. I felt disoriented and panicky—the way I once felt in a hall of mirrors when I was a kid, clamoring to find my way out. Later that summer, Millie said the doctors kept me after Noah died. They gave me a shot of something and wouldn't let me go home.

My parents and Nina appeared and Millie moved aside, making way for my mother, who took Millie's place beside me. She cradled and rocked me and stroked my hair. My father stood at the foot of my bed. He was crying, and clearing his throat to hide that he was—the same way he did at my wedding. Nina stood with Millie, their sobs muffled in an embrace. I buried my head in the pillow next to mine where Noah's head had lain beside me for the last six years, his wedding band clutched in my fist.

❧

I have never been to visit Noah's grave. I have thought about it over the years but what is the point of looking at a stone engraved with his name? I wanted to speak at the funeral but I couldn't. Noah's brother, Tim, gave the eulogy. My father was a pallbearer. There must have been a hundred people there: friends, relatives, professors, people from the restaurant—customers and staff. I wasn't the only person who loved Noah.

The day of the funeral my parents and Nina and I drove out to the house in Chatham. My eyes were shut as I sat in the back of the Roadmaster curled up beside my sister. I heard my parents' muted conversation in the front seat, felt the curves in the road and the warm sunlight through the windows and smelled the sea air as we approached the Cape. I felt Nina's arm tighten around me and I couldn't understand how it was possible to still have my senses since the better part of me died that Monday night with Noah.

CHAPTER THREE

Olivia

Had anyone asked me what the weather was like on the Cape
that summer, I wouldn't have been able to say. I barely knew
which days were sunny or cloudy, warm or cool. In August, before Nina went back to school, she and I ventured here and
there. Going out and about took Herculean effort on my part,
but Nina was relentless, insisting we both needed to get out of
the house. We drove Route 6A and stopped along Main Streets
in towns along the way, pretending to be tourists. Pretending to
be who neither of us were that summer.

Several times, we walked the beach at dusk and once, pre-
dawn, a friend of Nina's took us by boat to Monomoy Island
where we watched the sunrise. We stayed up until four in the
morning nearly every night those last two weeks before Nina
left for school. We went to the stationer and bought magazines
and bags of penny candy and lay on our stomachs the way we
did when we were girls, leafing through fashion pages in a
brave attempt to distract ourselves from reality with the added
brutality that, come September, we'd be apart.

Nina was in her last year at Mount Holyoke, and although
she tried to convince our parents that she could take off a se-
mester, they would hear "nothing of it." I heard my parents
talking in the kitchen late one night. They were drinking tea
laced with amaretto (their favorite nightcap) and mapping out

what my father referred to as my road to recovery, likening it to
the re-entry of soldiers after the War and the Reconstruction. He
had a plan: I needed to "move on" and "pick up the pieces." My
father had a dreadful habit of speaking in cliches. Maybe
Boston, he said. Close by. Not far from Nina. She can "come and
go" as she pleases.

She doesn't know anyone in Boston, my mother argued.
That's no solution.

She shouldn't be back in New York, my father said bitterly.
And, on that point, they agreed. My father suggested secretarial
school where I might learn a marketable skill like shorthand or
typing. She'll need to support herself, he said. And then my
mother asked how he could be so clinical, and began to cry. My
father's chair scraped the linoleum floor and his fist pounded
the counter. Damn it, Margaret, he said. What the hell do you
want me to do?

Until that moment, I had never thought about my parents in
terms of their marriage. I had only thought about them in terms
of parents whose relationship existed only as it related to Nina
and me. I hadn't stopped to think about the dynamic between
them, what they said to one another while they tended the garden or strolled on the beach together, or late at night when they
shut the bedroom door. By nature, children are selfish creatures.
The world revolves around them as they claw their way into
adulthood and, by the time they arrive, their parents emerge
merely as two people who, by happenstance, facilitated their
existence. Until, of course, children have children and then
everything changes. My mother's sobs subsided and my father
said "There, there, Meg," and I knew he was holding her. My
father was not such a tough old bird, despite the war stories
and the crusty veneer. And my mother, despite her brave attempts to paint the world with courage and determination, was
breakable.

I tiptoed upstairs to the room I shared with Nina, who was

sitting on the floor in a pile of sweaters, reluctantly folding them into a duffel bag.

"What?" Nina asked. Nina can look at my face for a split second and know something's wrong.

"I was eavesdropping on Mom and Dad."

"And?"

"Dad is planning my life. The soldier's road to recovery. Like the damn Reconstruction. And Mommy is crying."

Nina stopped what she was doing. "Crying? Oh, no."

Our mother didn't cry easily.

"I shouldn't be here," I said, folding a sweater. "I'm supposed to be a grown-up but I don't know what to do or where to go."

"Well, what is it you want?" The moment she asked, she visibly flinched.

"To be with Noah."

"Livi," Nina's face blanched. "I know. I didn't mean . . . "

"It's OK." I bowed my head and whispered. "I'm just not ready to be alone. Not yet."

"No one says you should."

"No, I know that. I just feel so pathetic. Like a coward. Sometimes when I'm falling asleep I literally feel myself falling and I jump and then I can't catch my breath. It's like it feels real one moment and there's some acceptance in me and then the next it's just a nightmare except I'm not waking up."

"Livi . . . "

I held up my hand. "See, if I stay here, I know that Mommy and Dad are down the hall." I felt panicky. "What would it feel like if I were completely alone?"

"Well, let's think. What could you do if you stayed here?" Nina asked, encouraging me.

It's hard to believe she was only twenty that summer. She had the patience and wisdom of an old soul.

I shrugged. "Waitress?"

"You're an actress."

I shook my head. "Forget that. I couldn't focus to memorize a line right now. But I'm thinking that maybe I can work for Dad." Our father owned a hardware store in town. "He always wanted to open a little gift section. Maybe I could do that. I mean, we could open in time for the holidays, you know?"

"Ask him," Nina said.

"What?" I was deep in thought, remembering holidays with Noah.

"Ask Dad."

"I will." I sat on the floor next to her. "When exactly do you have to be back at school?"

"September first."

"I want you to come with me to New York."

"What for?"

"To get my things. The security expires September first."

"Oh, God, Livi. Do you have to?"

"Yes, I have to. They're our things, Nina. How can you ask that?"

"You know, think about this for a minute. Your friends are in New York. You're sure you wouldn't be better off living—"

"Never," I said.

"I don't mean in the apartment," she said. "I mean in the city. Working with Dad—maybe that won't be the best thing. Your life was in Manhattan."

"Noah was my life. There's nothing there now." Nothing anywhere, I thought but didn't say.

She stood up from the pile of sweaters. "Of course, I'll go with you," she said, putting her arms around me.

And then we cried.

My mother came into our room early the next morning with Nina's laundry. It's funny how certain scents from childhood trigger memories. The laundry smelled like Arm & Hammer baking soda. I keep a box in the refrigerator and each time I inhale the scent, I am filled with a sense of safety and home and simplicity. She set the laundry basket on the floor and sat on the edge of Nina's bed. Nina was taking a shower.

"Mommy, Nina and I are going to New York on Saturday. To the apartment for my things. We have it all planned," I said, bracing myself for her reaction.

"Why can't we all go?" my mother asked cheerily. She began taking folded clothes from the basket and placed them on the foot of Nina's bed. "Really, I don't think you girls should go alone."

"Going alone with Nina will be easier for me."

My father came into the room just then. "Go where alone with Nina?"

"New York," I said.

"New York? What for?"

"To get her things, Henry," my mother said, as though it had been her idea.

"And there's something else. I heard you talking downstairs last night." I looked into my father's eyes. "I don't want to live in Boston. I don't want to go to typing school."

My father started to say something but my mother interrupted him. "Tell us what you want, Livi," she urged.

"I want to stay here for a while. Until I get settled. I'm not a good soldier, I guess."

My mother's eyes misted over and she took my face between her hands. "Of course, you can stay here," she said. "You don't have to ask."

"It won't be forever," I said.

"As long as it takes," my mother said. Her eyes were liquid pools. "Believe me, I understand."

I turned to my father. "I was thinking. Maybe I could open a little gift shop in the back of the store. I'll run it myself. I can do that, you know."

My father didn't speak. He placed his hand on my shoulder. It was his way of saying yes.

My parents are what people call hearty New England stock. Once, when I was a kid, I flew over the handlebars of my bike and ended up with ten stitches under my lip. My parents made me get back on the bicycle the next day and said I was lucky, that it could have been worse. My mother wasn't as hearty that summer. Her sorrow was nearly as great as mine. At that moment, as she held my face in her hands, it was all too apparent: While I grieved for Noah, she grieved for me.

On Saturday morning, my mother made salted cucumber sandwiches and filled a ribbed metal thermos with iced tea and placed them on the front seat of the Roadmaster. My father gave us a road atlas marked with colored circles and arrows mapping the way to New York City, a flashlight, a tire gauge, crude handwritten instructions for changing a flat, and an umbrella. Of course, they were unnecessary precautions—I'd made the drive from Chatham to New York dozens of times, and it was a clear day under a turquoise sky. The landscape was dappled with sunlight. I wondered how the day could be so perfect when the task that faced me was so grim.

We came into the city over the Triborough Bridge and down the FDR Drive. Nina drove us into the city. When we left Massachusetts I was the one behind the wheel, but as soon as we drove into New York State, we pulled onto the shoulder and Nina took over. Every mile that brought us closer to Manhattan took my breath away. When the Manhattan skyline rose before me, I shut my eyes.

We parked in a garage off Sixth Avenue, in deference to my parents, who gave us thirty dollars and made us promise to park in a garage and have a decent meal. Thirty dollars bought a lot back then. Ten dollars, a small fortune for Noah and me, paid for our dinner at Jefferson Market and a bottle of wine. Nina and I walked to the apartment carrying cardboard boxes that said CARNATION EVAPORATED MILK on the sides, and two gray suitcases from what my father called "the year one," the handles reinforced with black electrical tape.

There wasn't a wind stirring the air but as we got to the building a piece of paper floated down from the roof. It was half of a cocktail napkin that had LA TRATTORIA printed on the border. That was the restaurant where Noah and I worked. We had a small stack of those napkins tucked under a paperweight on our checkerboard table. I looked up, but no one was there.

Our landlady, Mrs. Rorimer, was expecting us. Noah had been her favorite tenant. He was the one who changed the fluorescent bulb on her kitchen ceiling and relighted the pilot light on her stove which she often suffocated by blowing on a spoon while tasting something from the pot. And he made her laugh. He called her Mrs. Roaring-More whenever she came to collect the rent check. She always said, "If you kids can't make the rent this month, I can wait a bit." But we always had the check and she never had to wait. When Nina and I walked up the stoop, Mrs. Rorimer was sitting at the top, fanning herself with a magazine. She stood and put her arms around me.

"You're a rail, dearie," she said. "Poor child."

It was the last thing I needed to hear.

It was, undoubtedly, a subconscious act that made me leave my house keys at home. Nina and I followed Mrs. Rorimer up the steps. She took the key tagged "Emerson" in shaky hands from a large ring attached to her belt and opened the door to the apartment. Although it had been unoccupied for nearly two months, I could swear it still smelled like vanilla. Noah loved vanilla anything and had a penchant for vanilla incense. Mrs. Rorimer explained that she had cleaned out the refrigerator and emptied the trash but didn't touch anything else. Noah's white Oxford work shirt hung on the back of the desk chair. There was a basket of our dirty laundry in the corner. Our robes were spread at the foot of our unmade bed, tousled from our lovemaking. The single white rose, now brown, drooped in the bud vase on the night stand. And the wall clock in the kitchen read eight-forty when life as I knew it had stopped.

I left a great many things behind that afternoon, taking only what mattered in terms of Noah and me. I left the furniture and plates and pots and pans, except for a black and white speckled lobster-type pot and a copper double boiler that had been my grandmother's. I wished I could have taken the mural from behind the bed. The herbs on the roof had burned in the sun and our little table and chairs were dusted with a thick coat of soot. Except for the suit Noah wore when we got married, his robe, a T-shirt, and a green cable knit sweater, I left his clothing. I took his guitar, and packed my meager wardrobe in one suitcase. I filled several boxes with books and records, peeled our Picasso poster from the wall, and wrapped trinkets from a shelf in the living room where Noah and I displayed the silly souvenirs we bought whenever we went anywhere. Snowglobes and plastic figurines and silvered spoons with enameled emblems on the handle. We hadn't been too many places—just Niagara Falls and the Statue of Liberty and an impulsive trip one August to Bar Harbor, Maine.

Nina ran down to Mrs. Rorimer's for the mail and came back with a Bonwit Teller shopping bag filled to the brim.

"So much!" I said. "What is all that?"

"Sympathy notes," Nina said grimly.

I opened one. *We are sorry for your loss and wish you strength and healing. Bob and Mary Franklin.* "Who are these people?" I turned the envelope over for a return address. "Brooklyn, New York."

"Probably family friends. I'll help you answer them," Nina said solemnly.

"Why would I answer them?"

She nodded. "You know. The way Mommy did when grandma died. You have to thank people for their sympathy."

I stared at her, crumpled the note and threw it on the floor. Anger is a better panacea than grief when it comes to survival.

"Some people just buy printed cards," Nina said patiently. "Then you don't have to write anything. You just sign them." She swallowed hard. "Or you don't have to bother. It's up to you."

"He could have left the liquor store that night," I said. "It wasn't like he was there and the robber came in and he was trapped. He could have turned and run when he saw what was happening. He could have gone for help."

"Livi, you don't know that . . . "

I shook my head. The week before, I had mustered the courage to call the detective in charge of the case and he was kind enough to send a copy of the report. He sent it to Millie and Millie sent it to me, so my parents wouldn't know what it was. "But, I do know," I said, telling her about my conspiracy with Millie. "There was an eyewitness. A pregnant woman was at the register when the gunman came in. He was pointing the gun at the clerk when Noah walked in. He saw what was happening. She was certain he would just turn and leave but he didn't. Noah tried to talk to the gunman. He said the clerk would give him the money and that he wouldn't have to shoot anyone and then he put out his hand, like he was trying to get the guy to give him the gun and that's when he was shot. And then the guy ran. No money. No liquor. Nothing. Some kids playing basketball on West Fourth stopped him." I could hardly breathe. "Why didn't Noah just leave? Why did he have to be some big fucking hero? How could he do this to us? He could have gone out the door and called the police. He was my whole world, didn't he know that?"

Nina just looked at me, tears streaming down her cheeks.

"I'll tell you why he didn't leave," I said as though she had asked, not even realizing I was crying as well. "Because that wasn't Noah. Noah believed that he could reach anyone. That he could reason with anyone. He thought that even people whose hearts appeared to be dark had something that could redeem them. He used to work at the Boys Club once a month when we were in college. Some of the kids were real troublemakers, you know? The guy who shot Noah was only sixteen. Noah didn't see a killer holding that gun. Noah saw a kid. That's why he didn't leave. Noah didn't turn his back on people." I looked up at her. "I want to go to the liquor store."

"Oh no. God, Livi, it's enough."

"You don't understand. I have to," I said.

Nina stopped arguing. She *did* understand. I needed to stand where Noah stood the last moments of his life, to walk through the same door and touch the doorknob. We retrieved the car from the garage, loaded it up, drove the short blocks over to Sixth Avenue and doubled-parked in front of the liquor store. A bell tinkled when I opened the door. I walked to the counter and stood before the clerk. His eyes were sad and rheumy and I imagined what they must have looked like when they were fearful and looked into Noah's.

"How can I help you, miss?" he asked.

At first, I couldn't speak.

"Miss?"

"My husband was killed here in July," I said.

He took my hand tightly, sandwiched in his palms.

Tears rolled down my cheeks. "I need to know what happened."

The man shook his head.

"Please," I whispered. "You have to tell me."

"He told the boy to give him the gun. I told him I would just give him the money. He told the boy he would ruin his life. Your husband put out his hand and stepped toward him and the gun fired. Everything happened so slow. I went to your husband." He pointed at the floor beside me. The wood was darker in one spot and I knew it was stained with Noah's blood.

"He was conscious?"

The man nodded. "I told him to be still. He tried to speak. He said what sounded like 'live.' I thought he was telling me that he would live, that he would be OK."

"My name is Olivia," I said.

The last word Noah murmured was my name.

It was after midnight when Nina and I got back to Chatham. We stopped once along the way at a diner and I forced myself to eat a grilled cheese sandwich and drink a Coca-Cola. My parents waited up for us and came outside as we pulled up the driveway. My father said we could unload in the morning but the look on my face prevailed upon him and we all unloaded the car in silence, each of us carrying boxes one by one to the attic where my father had cleared a space in a corner by one of the dormer windows. My mother had gone into town that morning and bought an old trunk that she relined with blue calico. She said it occupied her for most of the day as she scrubbed the inside with bleach and cut and glued the fabric.

My mother stayed with me while I filled the trunk, her hand pressed on the small of my back as she knelt beside me. The lid on a box of letters wouldn't close. I opened it to see why and found the popsicle stick windmill that Noah made for me the night before we married.

"What's that?" my mother asked.

"His wedding gift to me."

"A windmill?"

I nodded. "He loved them. He loved the Navajos. One day we planned to go to Arizona and walk the canyons. We thought maybe next July. Canyon de Chelly. That was one of Noah's dreams." I put the windmill in my mother's hands. "The Navajos believe that people have to pass through three different worlds before they can emerge into the present. That each person has a wind within them and it gives them the power to breathe and talk and move and think. Noah said that we'd always ride the wind together."

"Don't you want to keep that windmill with you, Livi?"

"No," I said, taking it from her hands and placing it in the trunk.

"Oh, Livi, why? We need our memories. They're so precious, Livi."

I shook my head. I didn't want memories. I wanted the real thing.

It was just the two of us in that dusty attic. For a moment she wasn't my mother. She was another woman, someone's wife, who felt the pain in my heart. But as soon as I felt myself begin to dissolve, she became my mother again.

"Tell me this isn't real," I said.

"You're going to be all right," she said, rocking me. "You'll see."

"How do you know?"

"Because I do," she said, smoothing the hair back from my forehead.

I shut the lid of the trunk.

"One day. You'll see, Livi. One day. I promise you."

And at that moment I wanted so badly to be a child again and believe unequivocally in her omniscience.

My mother and I closed up the attic and joined Nina and my father on the porch before we retired for the night. It was a bit cool so we bundled in sweaters and shawls. My mother made a pot of cocoa and we warmed our hands over the steaming mugs. My father remarked that the night was so still, not even a breeze. Just at that moment the wind chimes hanging from the porch beam tinkled ever so softly.

"Did you hear that?" I asked.

"Hear what?" they asked in unison.

"Nothing," I said, touching Noah's wedding ring that I wore around my neck. I thought of the napkin wafting from the rooftop earlier that day. I knew he was there with me and always would be.

I thought back on all this as I sat on the dock after Carl was first gone. The clouds parted as a breeze blew through the night, revealing a mottled, not-quite-full moon. I'd been on the dock for hours.

"Time to go," I said to Emmet who stood at the words.

As I walked up the hill to the house, I peered over the ridge hoping Carl's car might be in the driveway and this would all be over. He would explain and the reasons would be simple and uncomplicated. But his car wasn't there and the house was dark. I did Carl's chores: He was the one who turned on the lights at nightfall and turned them off at dawn, checked the old gas burners on the stove, let Emmet out at night and, made the morning's coffee.

I went upstairs to our bedroom and pictured Carl naked, crawling into bed beside me, taking me in his arms with the quiet acquiescence that always brought us together in the darkness. Carl and I never made love in daylight. We never spoke. We made love in silence yet I longed for the unspoken words.

I lay in bed and had a sense of Carl that frightened me as intensely as it had years ago when I felt myself falling in love with him—something I swore I would never do again since loving leaves us too bare and vulnerable.

And, there I was, twenty-five years later, still listening to the wind.

CHAPTER FOUR

Carl

The morning I left, I showered and shaved and put four hundred dollars in my wallet that I had stashed away over the last year or so. A dollar here, five dollars there. It was something I got in the habit of doing since I was ten years old when I dreamed of taking my Mama and heading out someplace where we'd have a house and a yard with a white picket fence and it would be just the two of us. Instead, when I was seventeen, I ended up heading out alone. I have wrestled with demons for forty-one years. They've taunted me, asking me if I made the right choice.

I've often thought about what people say after a man they know has gone on a drunken spree or committed a crime. How people say he was the best neighbor, husband, father, friend . . . and conclude that "he certainly wasn't who we thought he was." Someone could have said that about me and been as right as rain.

It was gratifying not to make the turn into campus that morning as I had for the last thirty years, although I wasn't certain if I still had the nerve I had at seventeen. If the impulse to return wouldn't be seduced by the lure of the comfortable, familiar, and safe. But impulses happen so quickly that we just can't stop them—even when we're older and they come a little slower than they used to.

At seven-thirty, I crawled into the morning rush on Interstate 91. The driver in the car behind me was drinking coffee from one of those thermal aluminum mugs and talking on his cell phone. Probably talking to his wife. Complaining, as he probably did every morning, about the bumper-to-bumper traffic, outlining his day, asking her what she's planning for dinner. How I envied what I guessed was his uncomplicated, ordinary life as he made his way along the highway. He exited in front of me, his short commute. Mine was eight hundred miles away.

For most of my life, the world knew me as a professor of physics. Married. Two children. My wife, Olivia, is an actress. She teaches drama now but, in her heart, my wife is an actress. When I first met Olivia, she had long brown hair and looked not a year over eighteen even though she was well into her twenties. It was her eyes that drew me in, so filled with emotion, reflecting mine in a way that no one could see. She wears her hair cropped close to her face now. She cut it a few months ago, just before she turned fifty, because she read that short hair makes a woman look younger. The joke is that scientists are socially inept—fools who can only see things when magnified through a microscope—but the words were on the tip of my tongue as she twirled in front of me with her new look. Instead of saying she didn't need to look any younger—instead of saying she looked beautiful—I said nothing.

Words unsaid were my problem. There were many times I longed to confess to her, to tell her what happened to me at seventeen, but I never knew where to begin or how the story would end. I even planned the moment when I would take her down to the river and sit on that spot she likes so much on the dock. I would hold her hands in mine and look into her eyes and tell her who I was and who I had tried to become—and hope she would love me not only in spite of what I told her, but because of it all as well. There were walls between Olivia and me and I feared that destruction would be the only result if they came tumbling down.

There were many things I should have told my wife. Like how she felt beneath me in the darkness. How there was no sense of "me" anymore but rather just the two of us as I held her in my arms and looked into her eyes. I never told her how it felt with her skin pressed against mine or how privileged I felt to be allowed what was forbidden to all but me. I never told her how much I loved her.

Memories haunted me, depleting my strength when I was awake and tormenting me as I tried to sleep. The specters had become increasingly relentless and unforgiving. And then the boy came into my office that Monday.

"Professor Larkin? My name's Robbie Martin." He shook my hand. " I need to ask a favor, sir," he said in a soft southern accent that took me to another life.

I waved him into my office and the chair in front of my desk.

"There's this woman who took care of my grandma her whole life and, well, sir, I'm pretty close to her myself. She watched over me and my sister sometimes when we were little. Anyway, my father called this morning and the lady had a heart attack." His face turned red and he became visibly emotional. "I want to go home and see her, sir. I keep thinking, what if she passes before I . . . Anyway, sir, I have my lab on Thursday morning but I can be back by afternoon. I checked on the flights and the connections already. I thought I could make up the lab with the other class. They have theirs at four on Thursday. See, she's like a grandmother to me, sir."

"How far away is home, Mr. Martin?" I asked, the cynic in me thinking this was one of the more imaginative postponement excuses I'd ever heard from a freshman who was overwhelmed with Physics 101. He was nearly entertaining.

"North Carolina, sir."

My heart stopped. "I see. Well, that's quite a journey."

"The only rough part is from Raleigh-Durham into Warrensville—that's my hometown—but my folks'll pick me up at the airport and if all goes well, it's only a two-hour drive."

"Warrensville," I said numbly.

"You know it, sir? Right there on the Thunder River."

"I don't, I'm afraid." I removed the thumbtacked lab schedules from my bulletin board. "Well, I don't see the harm in that. The lab you want will be in Room Eight, Rumson Hall."

"Yes, sir. Thank you, sir. I really do appreciate this."

"What's the lady's name, Mr. Martin?"

"Mary Lou Parker."

I said nothing. I just stared at him.

"You can check with my folks, sir, if you like. I know this sounds bogus but, honestly . . . Sir?"

"No, Mr. Martin, it's fine. And I wish her all the best. Have a safe trip. We'll see you back here on Thursday."

I barely slept that entire week until the boy came back most reliably on Thursday at two o'clock. I heard him ask for me and opened my office door.

"Mr. Martin," I greeted him. "Welcome back. I hope all is well."

"She's doing just fine, sir, thank you for asking. My mother calls her the unsinkable Mary Lou."

"Well, you must be very relieved," I said.

"Yes, sir. Thank you, sir."

"I take it she's at a hospital in Raleigh?"

"You know the area, sir?"

I felt my face redden. "I have friends, colleagues, down at UNC."

"Oh, right. Well, no actually, Miss Parker's at a cardiac care facility about thirty minutes out of Warrensville in Leland but the doctors say she'll be out of there in no time."

"I hope she doesn't live alone."

"She lived with my grandma until a few years ago, but when my grandma passed, we set her up in one of those assisted-living facilities. This place has been real good for her. They have activities and she's got friends. She has no family herself. She's been alone as long as we've all known her."

"She has quite a family with all of you." My response was a well-practiced exercise in self-control.

"That she does. And thank you again for your kindness, sir," he said.

His soft southern voice rang through me like a melody. I could have listened to him for hours. That was when I knew that despite what I had buried, I never forgot the song.

৯

I could have been in Warrensville hours earlier than I arrived but I stopped for a sandwich and coffee and took a nap by the side of the road since I'd barely slept the night before. The pines appeared silver in the moonlight and a wind tipped them to their sides, beckoning me down River Road.

I have tried to believe that I am a physicist and feel the science with every ounce of my being. I could tell you about the laws of nature and why things happen the way they do. About actions and reactions and why certain occurrences are meant to be and others are a scientific impossibility. As a young man, when I first came to Belvedere, I lectured the first-years about the wind, perhaps the most fundamental equation there is when talking about energy: Wind speed defines the distance that wind travels divided by the amount of time it takes for wind to travel that distance. I waxed on. Lecturing. The wind is not reliable, however, when it comes to energy. You can only harness its power in the horizontal direction of motion. If you have a sort of vector to measure its force, the blades can only turn on one axis. You can't really predict the strength of the wind, so how can you decide how heavy or light to make the weight of the blades? Oh, but once my perception of life was different. There were face values and visceral reactions and simpler answers where pines bent in the wind without formulas.

After Robbie appeared, I realized that formulas had failed me. I had abandoned religion a long time ago and decided that faith was for the weak and nothing but false comfort. And just when I thought I had everything figured out, I wished for faith again—or perhaps I was confusing faith with truth. I came to realize that truth could not be altered with any success, no matter how much I tried to forget, justify, and pretend.

On the street where I lived as a kid, there was a cottonwood next to a climbing rose in what was a poor excuse for our backyard. It was mostly sand and gravel. Well, one particularly rainy spring, the cottonwood and the rose grew so lush and out of control that they wrapped around each other and nearly strangled. Unlikely bed partners, Mama said, as she cut them apart before they suffocated each other. And I wondered if, for even a moment, she was thinking about my father as she used those big shears to cut the brambles apart with such a fierce determination. I have woven webs more tangled than the cottonwood and the rose. Oscar Wilde said that truth is never pure and rarely simple. For sure, truth eventually sucks you up like quicksand and leaves you screaming and scrapping your way to the surface if you try to run. Truth catches up to you.

I drove through the familiar streets of Warrensville and wished my life had taken a different course. Of course, Mama used to say that if wishes were horses, beggars would ride.

CHAPTER FIVE

Olivia

Whenever I think about growing up on Cape Cod, I remember the winters. Depending on how you look at them, Cape Cod winters can be either dreary or a welcome respite from summer. Most "Capies" are relieved come the end of the season. The bars are no longer knee-deep with drunk tourists who've tried to keep up with the "townies." They've sobered up, put on their suits, and gone back to the real world. The end of summer brings back the normalcy of everyday life. Normalcy. A word permanently deleted from my lexicon ages ago.

I've always loved the Cape in winter. Even the winter on the Cape after Noah died gave me a sense of comfort. The steel gray sky was a magnet for the tide, the cove protected me, and the moorings rocked the harbor like a lullaby. The "summer people" are fooled into thinking that Nantucket Sound is more tender "in season," but those who live there year-round know better. The Cape is a great barrier against the more brutal winters suffered by the rest of Massachusetts. On winter days when the sky is azure, even the beach can trick you into believing it's summer again. Of course, that first winter after Noah died, I knew it was merely an illusion. His death was the last deception, the ultimate betrayal. I went through the motions of living as though hypnotized. The ability to distract myself left me. Nothing captured my attention. At my mother's insistence, I ate for sustenance. Every word I spoke was forced. I listened to my shallow breaths in the middle of the night, amazed to have respiration and a still-beating heart.

The first frost after Noah died came early in the season, the first week in October. The lavender mums lining the porch steps finally succumbed and wilted. My father clipped the plants to the root and brought the pots aside. My mother covered the outdoor lights with orange film for Halloween and I knew the long winter was coming. She tried to cheer me with reminiscences of winters when they took Nina and me to The Provincetown Inn in January—asking me if I remembered the swimming pool and bowling alley. But I was no longer a child and there were no more distractions.

I searched my soul for pockets of comfort, telling myself that one day I would think of Noah in a way that gave me solace instead of pain, and then panicked at the thought that healing might cause him to fade from my memory. The pain of loving a specter tortured me. My face was shadowed and I didn't think there would ever be a day when my reflection would show even a hint of contentment, let alone joy. I missed him. I missed him so much I ached inside, and nothing stopped the ache.

I don't know how I made it through that first year other than the fact that the resilience of the human spirit is astounding. My father agreed to open a section of the hardware store for gifts. The shop was my salvation, giving me no choice but to focus on numbers and inventory to maintain what my father let me start in good faith. I worked late hours to the point of exhaustion, a necessary state in order to sleep. My mother taught me to crochet, a pastime that occupied me but when I finished an afghan meant for my father's Christmas present, I was surprised to see that no two rows had the same number of stitches and my mother, although typically a stickler for detail, never corrected me.

My sense of time was skewed, not only by feelings of unreality as I battled the nightmare that had become my life, but the schedule for the shop was out of sync as well: In October, I bought Christmas cards and shopped around craft fairs for crocheted pot holders, hand-painted trays and trivets, spoon rests, silvered picture frames, and stuffed velveteen animals. Come November, I was buying valentines, and then Easter baskets and stuffed bunnies in February. I was never in the right season.

Seven months after Noah died, on Valentine's Day, Nina announced that she was in love with a man named Frank Jensen, and he was, and is, one of the nicest people I have ever met. For years, I marked most events by placing them in a chronology that fell into "time after Noah died." It wasn't until after I was pregnant with Sophie that I stopped. It was only then that I counted days into my pregnancy, looking through picture books that showed what the baby looked like at six weeks and three months and six months—so transparent at first, then fingers and toes and a life inside me.

I was happy for Nina, but the notion that she was in love and beginning a life with Frank made me lonelier and compounded my hopelessness. In August, Frank gave Nina a small round diamond and, a few days later, they came to Chatham and we celebrated with champagne.

Noah proposed to me on the carousel in Central Park.

"See if you can catch the brass ring," Noah said as I sat behind him on the painted horse.

"There is no brass ring. Not really," I said.

"Close your eyes," he said. And then he took my hand and slipped a wedding ring on the ring finger of my right hand. "Please be my wife, Olivia Hughes."

I opened my eyes and began to cry and laugh at the same time.

"You can move the ring to the left hand after we're married, OK? I'm sorry it's not a diamond . . . "

I kissed him. "I wouldn't want a diamond."

After the champagne, Nina and Frank walked on the beach

and my father went to his den and fell asleep in the easy chair. We'd used my grandmother's champagne flutes that night for the toast.

"What made you bring out these glasses?" I asked, as my mother rinsed one over a rubber mat she'd set in the kitchen sink.

"Because it was time," my mother said. "What's the point of having something beautiful if you're not going to use it?"

"You were always so afraid they'd break."

"Was I? Well, it's silly to have pretty things in storage when we can enjoy them. We'll just be extra careful, that's all."

I picked up a glass and ran my finger along the gilded rim. "You think you're so clever, don't you?" I asked.

"Why is that?"

"Because you did this on purpose. You used grandma's glasses to make a point."

"What point?" my mother asked, the glass in her hand suspended.

"That I can't live my life scared."

"That's ridiculous."

"I don't believe you."

"Olivia, is this going to be one of those situations where I have to defend myself? Because to tell you the truth we've had a lovely evening and I don't want to argue."

I had become difficult. Belligerent and somewhat bitter. Angry at the world, and my mother was the easy scapegoat. I found myself snapping at her for no apparent reason. She began taking a sterner posture with me. A combination of desperation, emotional fatigue, and what, nowadays, they call "tough love." Or maybe it was her idea of throwing some kind of symbolic ice water in my face.

"I am so scared," I whispered, the words tumbling from my mouth as I cried. "I'll never stop missing him," I felt an extraordinary sense of relief as I confessed.

My mother set the glass on the table beside me and covered me with her arms.

"What's going to happen to me?" I asked. "I'll never love anyone else."

"Don't say that, Livi. I know that's how you feel, but don't say that."

"Why? It's true. Never! Just never! How would you know?" My temper flared and I gestured with my hand knocking the flute off the table. I tried to catch it but only the broken stem remained in my hand.

My mother gasped. "Did you cut yourself?"

"No, Mommy, I'm sorry. I didn't mean to."

My mother's eyes filled with tears.

"Mommy, I said I was sorry." I sounded like a child.

"I don't care about the glass," she said. "It's not the glass, Livi."

She didn't have to say that it was I who was shattered. I only came to understand my mother's despair when I became a mother. At the time, I thought her determination to make me whole again was to ease *her* pain, bring normalcy back to *her* life. I came to realize that it was only and entirely about me. She had her husband and her children and her home. She had the promise of Nina's future with Frank. My mother wanted me to have a second chance. It tormented her that I couldn't look to the future. It would be a safe guess to say she had lain awake many nights wondering if I would be a long-in-the-tooth old woman working in my father's gift shop. For me, the thought of loving anyone again was unbearable.

Some nights I prayed that Noah would come back to me in the guise of someone else, apologizing as I prayed, since, long ago, I disavowed religion, reducing it to something divisive and false. I even questioned, superstitiously, if Noah's death was my punishment for lack of faith.

Thinking about the future at all overwhelmed me with guilt. Daring to think of another husband, another man's children, was sacrilege. Besides, I no longer had the courage to live any sort of life. I would always be waiting for something to happen. How could I say good-bye to a husband in the morning and watch him get into his car and drive to work and feel certain that he'd make it home that night? Or watch my children play in the yard, fearing that if I turned my back for a moment they might disappear? When they got a fever or a bellyache, I would assume it was something far worse, something insidious and life-threatening. I would never be like my mother who could glance at the clock when my father was late coming home and say, "Now, wherever can your father be? Supper's getting cold."

For me, someone would always be on the brink of vanishing in the night.

It's a strange thing about losing a husband. You remain defined as a daughter, a sister, a mother, and a friend when those who give you the definitions are gone. But when you lose your husband, you are no longer a wife. In the blink of an eye, you become a widow. A fragment left dangling, undefined, and alone.

CHAPTER SIX

Olivia

It was no surprise the following June when Millie's wedding invitation arrived. She and Tom had been engaged for years—long before Noah and I married. I was the first of our "group" to get married and the first, at twenty-five, to be widowed. Weddings and even baby shower invitations came on a regular basis. There was a cruelty to it all and yet it was to be expected. I sent gifts but declined all invitations except for Millie's.

The October wedding was in Boston. That was the night I met Carl. It was the weekend that a hurricane skirted the Carolinas and left its spoils along the east coast, stopping for one last blustery surge in New England. I managed to get a cab for the few short blocks from my hotel on Huntington to the restaurant on Newbury where Millie was having her rehearsal dinner.

Carl and I spun through the revolving door at the same time and met again at the coat check. His trench coat was drenched and his umbrella had turned inside out. His long dark hair that hung well over his shirt collar was soaked as well. In those days, he held his back and broad shoulders straight, with that cocky posture of youth. Now he is slightly slouching with the burden of age and, I suppose, just living. He apologized to the woman behind the coat check as he handed over his wet trench coat and turned to me.

"Some night," he said, combing back his hair with his fingers. "I couldn't get a taxi. You look like you had better luck."

"I did," I said, taking my coat check. "It's supposed to storm like this all weekend."

A waiter walked past with a tray. "Which room is the dinner for Millie Benson?" I asked.

"Dove Room," Carl answered before the waiter. "I'm here for the rehearsal dinner, too."

"Oh?"

"Carl Larkin," he said, extending his hand. "Friend of the bride."

"Me, too," I said, shaking his hand. "Olivia Emerson. Millie's my best friend."

Why hadn't Millie mentioned this man?

Carl read my mind. "Actually, I'm more a friend of the bride's father."

"Are you a biologist?"

"Physicist, but we science types stick together. I teach at Belvedere College in Willow. Lloyd was one of my professors from way back when at MIT," he said as we walked to the Dove Room.

"Ah." I didn't know what to say.

Everyone was gathered around the bar. Millie ran over to me. "I'm so glad you're here," she whispered, hugging me. "I was afraid you might not come."

"Only for you," I said.

Carl headed for the bar, greeting Lloyd along the way, kissing Millie's mother, Patricia. I scanned the receiving table—only four name cards remained, among them Carl's and mine. Our table number was the same.

"We meet again," he said, as he sat beside me and set his martini down on the table. "Can I get you something from the bar?"

"Why do they put olives in martinis?" I asked, peering into his glass.

"Flavor. Some people like onions. Olives are more traditional."

"Why three?"

"Supposed to be good luck. Like three coffee beans in sambuca."

"I never had one."

He held the glass out to me. "Taste?"

I shook my head. "No, thanks." I lifted my glass of ice water. "This is fine for now."

"So, tell me how you know Millie."

"From college." I wasn't used to casual conversation with anyone but customers.

"She teaches English, doesn't she?"

I nodded.

"Do you also teach?"

I shook my head. "No."

"Do you live here in Boston?"

"Cape Cod. Chatham." I knew I should ask him something as well. At best, he would think I had no personality. At worst, I was being rude. "You?"

"In Willow. It's a little town about an hour from here. I teach at Belvedere College. Physics."

"Oh, right, you said that before."

"Well, it's not too memorable. Have you heard of Belvedere?"

"No."

"It's a small liberal arts college with a small undergraduate physics department." There was an uncomfortable silence. "OK, I give up. I think I've about used up my twenty questions. What do you do?"

I was embarrassed. "I'm an actress, I guess."

"You guess? Don't you know?" He laughed.

"I auditioned for a while but I didn't get anything," I said shyly. "Saying I'm an actress is better than saying I'm a waitress, which is how I used to make a living. Now I manage a gift shop." I twirled my hair around my fingers. "It's in the back of my father's hardware store."

"I've waited tables. It's hard work." He was gentle with me. "Where did you work?"

"New York City."

"Well, now, that must have been something. I was out in Kansas—mostly at barbecue pits."

"You're from Kansas?"

"No, I went to school out there. Undergrad."

"Why physics?" I asked.

"Why acting?"

I didn't like it when people answered questions with questions.

"Because I loved it. I loved transporting myself to another world and becoming someone else."

"Past tense?" he asked. He suddenly appeared uncomfortable.

"I'm not sure," I said. "Acting just isn't on the agenda right now."

I saw Carl the next night at the reception. We sat at separate tables, clearly either an oversight or a social gaffe on behalf of Patricia Benson. Despite her status as Boston socialite extraordinaire, Carl and I were the only "singles" at our tables.

Couples hit the dance floor and I sat alone, watching and wishing I were someplace else, preferably in my bedroom back on the Cape. Millie was glowing and beautiful. She looked like every bride I'd ever seen in the magazines. She looked the way I had felt just five years before at my own wedding.

There must have been at least three hundred people at the reception but, as I looked around the room, trying to act casual since my table was bare, I caught Carl's eye. He was also sitting alone. He waved and gestured toward the dance floor. I shook my head but he walked toward me.

"You'll make a fool of me if you turn me down. People are

watching. We're the only people not dancing." He whispered, "We'll look like rejects."

He made me laugh. "Oh, anything but that," I said. "We need to save face."

"Absolutely," he said and took my hand as I stood from my chair.

The music stopped just as we pushed our way onto the dance floor. I shrugged and began to walk away, grateful to be off the hook but the band struck up another number. A slow dance, and he took my elbow.

"Come on," he said, coaxing me.

I held myself stiffly.

"You're nervous," he said sympathetically. "Why? Don't be."

"I haven't danced in a while," I said self-consciously.

"Me neither, but no one's looking." He pulled me in closer and Noah's wedding band caught on a button on his shirt.

"Sorry," he said, untangling the ring. "What's this? A wedding band?"

"It's my husband's," I said, tucking it into my dress.

He stopped dancing and looked around the room. "I had no idea. I apologize. Where . . . ?"

"I'm a widow," I said.

"You're so young," he said.

The music played but we stood still.

"So was he. He died fifteen months ago."

"How are you?" he asked.

"What?"

"I said, 'how are you?' "

I looked at his face. Until that point my head had been down. "OK," I said.

"No, you're not," he said, and his face looked so sad. "Not a great place to be right now, is it?"

"What do you mean?"

"At a wedding." He paused. "Or anyplace at all."

I nodded my head. Don't start crying, I thought. Whatever you do.

"I can only imagine," he said.

"You don't want to," I said, surprised at the acerbic tone in my voice.

We finished the dance and I thanked him.

"You know what?" he asked, stopping me before I got back to my table. "There's a great little bar in this hotel. How about we sneak away for a bit?"

"I don't think so. It wouldn't be polite."

He looked around the room. "Well, let's see. The way I figure, we've already had the rubber chicken entree and the cake's not going to be cut for at least an hour."

"How do you know that?"

"I have a hotline to the maître d'."

"No, you don't . . . " I couldn't help but smile.

"Come on, no one's going to miss us. I promise we'll be back in time for the toasts and the cake. What do you say?"

I nodded. "OK."

"Good. Now, I think it's high time you learned to drink a martini."

I scrunched up my nose. "Not a chance."

Most people tended to avoid me in those days as if tragedy was contagious or I was cursed with bad luck. Most people's knee-jerk response was to say they were "sorry" and I hated that expression the most since it seemed to implore me to comfort them as well. I felt, in so many ways, that my widowhood made me somewhat of a pariah since I never got one call or letter coaxing me to join festivities I'd declined for obvious reasons. Carl's reaction to me wasn't like that. My grief didn't scare him off.

The hotel bar was dark, with small round tables lit with candles in blue jeweled jars. The walls were papered in mottled red velveteen. Carl ordered two martinis and laughed when I sipped and sputtered.

"It tastes like cough medicine," I said. "How can you drink these?"

"It's an acquired taste," he said. "Take another sip. You'll see."

Halfway through, the drink went down easy. "These are nice," I said, just the slightest bit giddy as the drink went to my head.

"There you go. Told you so." He smiled.

"So, what's his name?" he asked in present tense.

"Noah," I said, knowing exactly whom he meant.

"What happened?" he asked. "Sometimes it helps to talk about it. Of course, if you prefer not to . . ."

"No, I'd like to," I said hesitantly.

"Was he ill?"

"I knew I shouldn't have worn mascara," I said, as a tear rolled down my cheek and when I wiped it my fingertip was black.

He handed me a cocktail napkin.

"He was murdered," I said.

Talking to Carl felt like a confession. I didn't tell him that Noah and I had just made love before he was killed or that Noah and I were celebrating his Broadway role. I didn't tell him about our rooftop garden or the mural on the wall behind our bed. I was making dinner, I said, and he'd gone out for a bottle of wine. The moment I heard the sirens, I knew they were for Noah. I didn't tell him that I kissed Noah as he lay on the gurney or how my blouse was covered with his blood. I didn't have to tell him how it felt when the doctor told me he was gone.

But I told him how I met Noah, racing around the corridor and dousing him with soda and the trick he played on me when it turned out that he was the TA. How Noah could spin the most dire of situations into something positive, that he played guitar and sang to me. That Noah was not only my husband but my best friend. That no one made me laugh the way he had and no one made me cry the way I did when he died. Carl listened intently, never taking his eyes from me. He sat nearly motionlessly, moving only to bring his drink to his lips. He never went to touch my hand. He never offered false words of comfort.

"It doesn't make any sense, does it?" I asked. "I keep trying to find a reason. It shakes my faith, you know?"

"That's why science is my drug," he said. "Action and reaction. It makes sense."

"Always?"

"No, not always, but when experiments fail, you just start over again and that's it. Very cut and dry. No one gets hurt— except maybe a researcher's ego now and then." He appeared distant for a moment. "Faith is too abstract for me. It's not reliable."

I changed the subject rather abruptly. "So, you went to school in Kansas. Is that where you're from?"

He studied my face. "I'm from the South," he said. "A little town in North Carolina called Matthew's Hill. Ever hear of it?"

I shook my head.

"Didn't think so. It's on the banks of the Thunder River."

"Why is it called Thunder River?"

"Well, let's see, probably because when the water gets high it rolls in like thunder," he smiled. "Something like that, I suppose."

That night was the first and last time Carl mentioned his hometown. His parents were killed in a fire just after his high school graduation. His parents had lit a kerosene lamp that caught the bedroom draperies and the house went up in flames. He had been visiting friends in Rocky Mount and when he came back on Sunday night, his parents were dead, the house was rubble and ash and he was seventeen and alone. He had a scholarship to UNC at Raleigh, but after the fire, he sold the land where the house once stood and drove all the way to Kansas. Matthew's Hill had too many bad memories. Everything they owned was destroyed: pictures, mementos, books.

Carl went through Kansas State on financial aid, did his graduate work at MIT on scholarship, and was offered a teaching position along with housing at Belvedere when he was twenty-five. It was too appealing to turn down given the loans he had to repay. He'd been at Belvedere for eight years at that point. I asked why he chose Kansas and he said that was where he finally got tired of driving, not to mention that the pickup was on its last legs.

He was nearly flat and emotionless, in some ways almost rehearsed, as he told his story. But then again, I was freshly widowed and Carl had been alone since he was seventeen. He had no brothers or sisters, no grandparents. I guessed that he had told the story many times over and, by then, it was part of his landscape.

"Have you been back home since then?" I asked.

Again, he answered my question with a question. "Didn't you say you could never live in Manhattan again?"

"I didn't grow up there, though. You must have old friends."

He looked uncomfortable. "People drift apart after a while. You know how it is—everyone's lives change after high school. People get married, have kids, move away."

"Not a soul? Not even an old girlfriend?"

"Not a soul," he said. "Oh, maybe an old girlfriend here and there. Sometimes I miss Kansas, though."

"Are you ever sorry that you left?"

"Oh, sometimes. Not really, though."

"Where do you feel you belong, though?"

"Most of the time?" He shook his head and smiled. "Nowhere."

"Me, too," I said.

There was an uncomfortable silence.

"So, what were their names? Your parents?"

"Deirdre and Martin." He looked at his watch. "I think the bride cuts the cake. We should go."

Until last November, I believed that Carl and I attempted to convince ourselves and fool each other into believing that we were content with Nowhere.

ی

I got back from Boston early Sunday morning and spent the day skimming through Christmas catalogues for the shop and cutting green and red felt for holiday shelves. Retail holiday schedules are crazy. I bought hobgoblins and witches in July and wreaths and Christmas ornaments in August. At least the business end of Christmas took my mind off the spiritual.

On Christmas Day, the year before, I had driven out Shore Road to the Chatham Lighthouse, leaving Nina and Frank and my parents rather distressed that I took off by myself. I'd been taking out library books on lighthouses, fascinated by the other-worldly legends that surrounded them, desperate to believe in another world or other dimension. Legend has it that a ghostly rider on a white horse comes out on stormy nights, swinging a lantern to lure mariners to their doom at the Chatham light. The light is automated now, but once there were light keepers living there with wives and children. Another Chatham light keeper had a wife and ten children and, tragically, while on Prudence Island in Rhode Island, his wife and youngest son were killed in the hurricane of '38. He remarried five years later and was quoted as saying that his wife was his "good companion" and looked after things. I wondered if that's what happens after we have our one chance at true love—if we just settle for pragmatism after that. Perhaps that would be my lot in life, to merely

be someone's "good companion," bear children, tend house . . .
No rooftops, no lovemaking, no romance. No breaking in two
when someone dies.

My father had yet another VFW meeting the Monday night
after Millie's wedding and Mom had dinner plans with Aunt
Harriet, who really is just Mom's best friend but she's known
me since the day I was born. Typically, I would still have been
at the shop but I was truly tired from the weekend.

"You should come with us," my mother urged. "You know, I
was certain you'd be working this evening, but we'd love to
have you."

"That's OK. It was a long weekend."

"There's some meat loaf and pecan pie left over from Sunday, " my mother said.

"I'll be fine."

"Livi, are you sure? I could just as easily stay home."

"Go!" I kissed her. "I'm going to take a hot bath and go to
sleep."

"I won't be late," she said. "I'll be back by ten. Maybe sooner."

She was nearly out the door when she poked her head back
inside. "There are some lovely lavender bath salts in the guest
bathroom."

The phone rang. "It's probably Nina," I said, finally shooing
her out the door.

"Have fun. Kiss Aunt Harriet for me." I grabbed the phone.

"Olivia Emerson, please," a man's voice said.

"This is she."

"Carl Larkin. You're not the easiest person to locate. I finally
asked Millie's mother for your number. I'd make a good detective, huh?"

I laughed. "A regular Dick Tracy," I said.

"How was your drive back? I thought it would never stop
raining."

"Not too bad. Lots of trees down, though. Well, not trees, really. Branches. Yours?"

"Other than a slight hangover, it was fine."

Silence. Not exactly a scintillating conversation.

"So!" I said, not knowing what to say.

"So, I'd like to see you again," he said.

"Oh, well . . ." I stammered.

"I can come out there. Unless, that is, you feel like taking a trip to scenic Willow. Actually, it's very pretty here. It's a three-hour drive for you, though. Something like that, I think." Clearly, he'd already calculated the distance.

He was self-conscious and I was no better. "Well, I think that Willow . . . it's awfully far . . . I don't think . . . I don't know . . ."

"I'd love to come out to the Cape," he said. "I always tell myself I should do things like that on the weekends and I end up staying in this apartment and grading papers. You'd be a perfect excuse."

"It's an awfully long drive for one evening."

"Are you discouraging me?"

"No, no, not at all," I answered, much to my surprise.

"Is there a place I can stay the night?"

I wasn't ready to offer him our guest room. "The Chatham Bars Inn is nice. Right on the ocean."

"Great, well, pick a restaurant and I'll be there on Saturday night around six."

"Well, OK."

"For an actress, you're not mustering up a lot of fake enthusiasm there," he said.

I laughed.

"I don't bite, Olivia. I enjoyed your company. I'd like to see you again. It's fairly simple."

"You need directions," I said, in a rather businesslike tone.

"Ready when you are," he said.

Nina called just as we hung up. "The line was busy," she said.

"A man I met at Millie's wedding called me. I think I have a date on Saturday night."

"You think or you know?"

"Well, he's coming at six. I gave him directions."

"Sounds like a date to me. What's his name?"

"Carl."

"And?"

"And what?"

"Last name? What does he do?"

"Larkin. He's a physicist."

"Huh, no kidding?"

"I don't know if I can do this."

"Do what?"

"We're supposed to have dinner."

"Well, let's see," Nina said. "You've had dinner before."

"Nina, you know what I'm saying."

"Livi, for God's sake, it's only dinner unless you want it to be something more."

"Of course, I don't want it to be more."

"Why not? You're not being unfaithful, Livi. You know that, don't you?"

I hated that Nina knew me better than I knew myself. I thought of the wind that tore through Boston the Friday night before and wondered if it was Noah's sanction or warning. I shuddered. Maybe the wind was just Noah reminding me that the power we shared couldn't even be weakened by death.

Carl and I had dinner at the Chatham Squire, steak and a bottle of red wine. We talked until well after midnight propelled by the differences between us: I was riveted by drama and symbolism and imagery and he was grounded by formulas and equations and, somewhere in the mix, there was a balance. I told him about the legendary rider and offered to take him to the Chatham light.

"Does this mean that you believe in ghosts?" he asked playfully.

"Until proven otherwise, why not?"

"There are scientific reasons for apparitions, you know," he said, explaining clouds and vapors and lights bouncing off the Sound that could account for what he called the "alleged haunting."

"You're no fun," I said, pretending to pout. "The ghost theory's better."

When we walked to the car, he took my hand and I let it rest in his. The unspoken bond we shared was indisputable: A boy of seventeen was not supposed to be an orphan any more than a woman of twenty-five should be a widow.

CHAPTER SEVEN

Olivia

Sophie is a junior at Berklee College of Music in Boston. She and her roommate rent an apartment in a two-family house in Brighton Center, which means she takes the bus home from campus, often at night, in inclement weather, and frequently alone. I wish she had opted for a more traditional campus with dormitories and no commute. For the first time, I understand my father's angst when I went to school in New York City.

When Sophie was four, she discovered my parents' piano in Chatham and Carl went out the next day and bought her a Baldwin upright at a garage sale. He had the bridge replaced and spent an entire weekend rubbing the wood with steel wool and polishing it with lemon oil. She played for years, nearly incessantly, until a violin became Sophie's passion. She plays Ravel with the same passion and fervor as she plays bluegrass. Carl says the kids must be throwbacks to some recessive gene. I can carry a tune at best and Carl has never even shown an interest in music, so Carl says a virtuoso is buried someplace in our genomic past. Once I was about to say that Noah played guitar and then I remembered there was no biological link to Sophie. As for her brother, Daniel, perhaps there was a rebellious ancestor who was a fast draw in the wild west while preaching on a soapbox.

Every Saturday morning Sophie meets friends for breakfast

at a local bagel shop near campus and calls home around eleven o'clock. Of course, she calls home as well during the week, but the calls hinge on how life is going: If everything's smooth, the calls are less frequent, simply to touch base. If the road is rocky, my phone rings off the hook. One Saturday, several months ago, Sophie didn't call until nearly one and hadn't answered her cell. That was just a week after a tumultuous breakup with a new boyfriend had caused her to fail a test in theory. The call was, of course, only two hours late, but I twisted my hands the entire time, telling myself there was no need to worry, trying to calm myself as I envisioned horrific scenarios. When the phone finally rang, I nearly jumped out of my skin, convinced it wasn't Sophie but someone alerting me to the fact that something had happened to her.

That particular morning when Sophie called later than usual, she and her friends had met some "new" boys for breakfast and, naturally, I wasn't the first thing on her mind.

"You get so worried, Mom," she said. "It's not fair. I take very good care of myself. Sometimes you're just over the top."

"That's not true," I said, defending myself. "Not really."

"No! It is true," she argued. "I mean, really, Mom, think about it: What could happen? Besides, you'd hear if something did."

It has been a constant battle to shield my children from the neuroses I developed after Noah was killed. One day, I thought, I will tell them about Noah. I will tell them what I fear could happen again. How a man I loved went to a store not two blocks from home and never returned. My children only know that my first husband died. They were young when I told them and my history before motherhood was irrelevant to them. They never asked questions. Young children equate husbands with fathers. My deceased husband had no place for them. So, how could I tell them how deeply I once loved another man? It would be a betrayal of their father, my husband—and we two were the unit that mattered in their world.

Of course, the Saturday after Carl disappeared, Sophie called promptly at eleven. I gathered myself and answered the phone.

"Hey, Mom."

What do I usually say? Do I ask how she is? Do I sound excited?

"Hi, sweetheart, I'm racing out the door," I said, calculating my response.

I lied.

"Where to?"

"Chatham."

Not a lie.

"With Dad?"

Don't hesitate.

"No, he's drowning in paperwork."

"Is he there? Can he say hello?"

"He's at the college."

She would never disturb him at the office.

"How come you sound weird?"

"It's your imagination."

"No, it's not." Sophie said, irritated. I take her moods personally, to heart, although Carl has always placated me by saying that they're merely manifestations of Sophie's artistic temperament. That morning, she was suspicious, I thought—unless it was my own paranoia because I wasn't telling whole truths. Sophie has the ability to read me as accurately as I read her.

"I'm just rushing. That's all. Will you be around later? I'll call you later."

"I'm going to the library."

"I'll call your cell. I love you, Sophie."

"Me, too, Mom. Bye."

She softens. She always softens. As do I.

Sophie is twenty. When I was three months pregnant, the

doctor placed a stethoscope in my ears and held it to my belly. It was magical—the alien rhythmic whooshing of my baby's heart beating with mine. Carl placed the stethoscope in his ears. A look of contentment and anticipation crossed his face, palpably flooding his being. "Life contagious," he said.

A few months went by and the doctor did a sonogram, presumably so we could see the growth of the baby and determine a more conclusive due date, but the doctor's face fell as she looked at the film. Sophie had a VSD, a ventricular septal defect, commonly known as a hole in the heart, and I remember wondering if it was genetic since there was an invisible one in mine. Carl's face turned a ghastly shade of gray. We went home that night and the more Carl tried to reassure me, interpret what the doctor explained about VSDs, how the hole typically closes by the time the child is a year old and then, if it doesn't happen naturally, a simple surgical procedure would remedy the problem, the more anxious I became. "My baby" and "simple surgery," an oxymoron in itself, were words unfit to even breathe in the same sentence.

Sophie was born without fanfare, a scheduled C-section gauged to prevent any problems with the VSD. She let go a bleating wail and, to the naked eye, she was perfect. She nursed and cried and turned pink and red and melted me with every gurgle, every sweet smile. She slept in a bassinet at the side of my bed for a year so I could listen to her breathe. She sucked my breast as I cradled her in my arms and I never believed the hole in her heart would heal. I spent the year waiting to lose her and the more Carl said we wouldn't lose her, the more I kept her to myself and Carl at a distance. I didn't want comfort or reasons or explanations. I just wanted my baby. What I didn't know at the time was that Sophie was my destiny, auguring what took me years to embrace—that a damaged heart can heal.

The hole closed on its own. Sophie became my miracle and

hope regained. She rescued me. She healed. Living, breathing proof that there was a future. After that, I never said good-bye without saying I love you. It was the same with Daniel and my parents and Nina. Everyone, except Carl. It was my own black magic, an acquired superstition: If I admitted that I loved him, something could take him away.

Daniel was born sixteen months after Sophie, fortunately unplanned, because I didn't have the strength or courage to have another child after what I went through with Sophie. He is not as communicative as his sister. Daniel doesn't call until Sunday nights when the weekend is out of his system. But, like Sophie, he can sense a difference or worry or angst in my voice when I simply say hello. For a long time, I attributed this to a sixth sense on the part of my children until it dawned on me that I was merely unsuccessful in keeping a tone from my voice when something was "wrong." Unlike Sophie, Daniel refuses to accept even the white lies. The lies of omission I have told over the years to shield my children from one thing or another. Once, when I had a lump in my breast, I lied. I was going to the breast surgeon but I said it was the dentist. What was the point of saying anything until the biopsy came back? As it turned out, there was nothing to tell: a benign cyst and about six others that would wax and wane if I cut down on caffeine and took vitamin E and that was the end of the story. Daniel sensed that I wasn't going to the dentist. He was only twelve but said I looked too nervous to be going to the dentist. When I told him the truth after the fact, he stormed off and slammed the door to his room, blasting his stereo as I pounded his door, pleading with him to hear me out. He refused until Carl intervened. Their relationship is odd: Despite what appears to be a lack of closeness, there is an underlying current of mutual respect, a nearly insidious simpatico that has always baffled me, although I find it gratifying.

Daniel opened the door with great resentment. He was not only angry, but frightened. If something had happened to me during surgery, he would never have said goodbye. They'd only given me local anaesthetic, I said, and his anger subsided. But all night long, he checked on me, poking his head in the door of my bedroom, asking if he could get me anything, if I was all right.

I was concerned that my lie of omission would be transparent to Daniel.

Daniel was always my mystery. Unlike me, because he is fearless, and unlike his father, who is apolitical and conservative. Daniel is passionate and rebellious, the champion of the underdog, taking up causes that he often solved, in younger days, with his fists. He spent more time in detention than the classroom. The fact that he's a freshman at Penn will never cease to amaze me. The joke was: Will Daniel get into Penn or the state pen? He is a conundrum of emotions, my Daniel, sweet, temperamental, unflinchingly honest, combative. He defends his beliefs with ardent, logical diatribes, eloquently and relentlessly forcing the opposition to retreat just for the sake of silence.

When Daniel was younger, he and Carl were oil and water. Since Daniel's away at school, their communication seems to be improving. Distance seems to give them a level of comfort. The phone provides a welcome barrier. I always sensed that Daniel's temperament scared Carl to death. When Daniel would come home from school, shirt ripped, lip bloodied, explaining that he was defending someone or something, thereby justifying his means, Carl retreated.

After Sophie's call, I made the bed and rinsed the coffee pot and, just as I was about to take Emmet for a walk, Nina called.

"You're out of breath," she said as soon as I said hello.

"Am I?"

"What are you doing?"

I didn't want to sound dramatic but I had to tell her. "Carl never showed up for work yesterday morning. He didn't come home last night."

"What?"

"He never went to work yesterday."

"Have you called the police?"

"They won't do anything for forty-eight hours."

"That's ridiculous."

"According to the detective, a mentally and physically competent adult is free to, well, take off for a while. Even married ones. He said they usually turn up after a couple of days."

"That's crazy. What if something happened to him?" She took a breath. "Livi, I'm sorry."

"He left a note."

"What kind of note?" she asked apprehensively.

"Not that kind."

Nina was annoyed. "Why didn't you say that in the first place? God, Livi."

"Because. Well, listen." I read it to her. "It doesn't really say very much."

"Do you think he's in some sort of trouble?"

"Carl? Don't be silly. Like what?"

"I don't know. Gambling? I don't know."

I had to laugh. "Gambling? Right, and Ginny places the bets for him."

Nina dropped her voice to a hush. "Do you think there's someone else?"

"You sound like the detective."

"Well, do you?"

"The wife's the last to know, right? Yes, I thought about it." I was getting impatient. "Nina, I just don't know. I don't know anything. But no. I don't think there's someone else."

"Listen, Jillian has a soccer game this afternoon but I can drive up this evening. She should be done around four."

"I'm going to Chatham," I said, tucking the cordless phone between my shoulder and ear as I ushered Emmet from the house.

"Does Mommy know?"

"Not yet. I'll tell her when I get there."

"But what if he comes home while you're away?"

"I'll have my cell phone."

"Aren't you worried?"

"Yes and no."

"If it were Frank, I'd be beside myself."

I thought for a moment. "I trust him."

"This isn't about trust. People don't just *leave*."

"I don't mean trust in the sense that I think he's either faithful or unfaithful. I just, I don't know, I have to believe he has a good reason. Carl doesn't do things without *reasons*."

"Do you think it's a family thing?"

"He has no family."

"How can you be so calm?"

"I'm not calm. Not really." Say it, I thought. Just say it. "Look, I can't let myself think that it's something awful."

"I understand," she said. "Call if you need me, will you?"

I sighed. "Don't I always?"

Emmet and I went back inside. I turned off the porch lights. They'd been on all night. I sat at the kitchen table, placed my head in my hands and called my mother.

"I thought I'd come over this afternoon," I said. "OK?"

"How nice! With Carl?"

"Just me. And Emmet, OK?"

"Where's Carl?"

"Oh, you know, him. Under a pile of papers. I should be there around five."

I packed a small duffel, poured Emmet's special diet into a

plastic bag, turned the porch light on again and left a note on the kitchen table.

Carl, I am in Chatham. Call when you get home.

I studied the note for a moment and added:

Love, Livi

CHAPTER EIGHT

Carl

It was well after dusk when I pulled into Warrensville. I was on the block where I once lived. There used to be a bus depot behind the house and I was surprised to see that it had been turned into one of those little strip malls with a pizza place, a Laundromat, and a video rental. I should have known things had changed when I drove past the new bus depot when I pulled into town.

My family was what people called across-the-tracks people, even though there was no train depot in Warrensville. But there was no term for people who lived near the Trailways. The buses rolled in and out of Warrensville every night of the week and twice on Saturdays and Sundays. In the summer heat, and when it rained, the smell of bus fuel filled our house so badly that even if Mama was baking a pie or cooking up okra or cauliflower, the stench was permeating. Sometimes Mama boiled cinnamon sticks and cloves and that helped for a bit but, all in all, it was pretty useless.

I drove around the block three times before I parked across the street from our old house. There never was a fire. The house was dim and the window shades, some of them cracked and yellowed, were pulled down. The covered front porch still had a single bulb in the same spot and I daresay whoever lived there now had never changed the fixture. There was a broken cane rocker and an old desk leaning against a broken spindle on the porch and the rusty chain-link fence that separated the house from the one next door was overgrown with honeysuckle. Mama used to have a patch filled with bright red poppies until the sheriff rang the bell one day and said the flowers were illegal because of the potential for heroin and Mama asked him what heroin was. He told her and she pulled the flowers out by the roots, saying she couldn't imagine how anything so magnificent could be outlawed, let alone lethal.

I was shocked to see that the house was so small and sat on pilings. Not that I ever thought it was large, but it wasn't more than eight hundred square feet and the yard was the size of a thumb print. To tell the truth, it hardly looked like much more than a trailer. The window to my old room faced the strip mall and I pictured the bare wood floor, the single bed—a pin-striped mattress on coiled metal springs—and sheet music and books piled ceiling-high in the corner.

I probably sat across from the house for a good ten minutes before I drove the familiar streets into town. Everything was changed and built up. Warrensville had always been a beach town, but it was apparent that it had become more of a resort town, hopping in the summertime. The red-brick guest walk by the river had been redone and, even on that cool November day, a couple rode in a horse-drawn buggy decorated with plastic flowers, bundled together under a rough wool blanket.

I thought about making the turn on Main, taking the sharp left at the light, and heading toward the beaches. It felt like yesterday when I would drive to that music club called The Factory down in Seaside where the black musicians played. Whites weren't allowed but sometimes I sneaked in just to listen, standing in the way back by the door. Sometimes I just sat outside in my truck with the engine running, straining my ears. It was an amazing place. Out of time. All those little juke joints with live music and people dancing all night long, from Friday night after work until church on Sunday morning. It was the black oasis back then. Blacks weren't allowed in the town library or at any of the so-called cultural affairs in Warrensville. Christ, they weren't even allowed in the five-and-dime. Some people admitted there was an invisible line drawn down the center of the town and others outright pretended the line wasn't there at all, but the division was plain as day. And if you crossed that line, whether you were black or white, you risked your life.

I met Laura in Seaside. I was sitting in my father's truck, listening to the music, smoking a cigarette, the window open, when she came up to me.

"You must be a crazy boy," she said. "What do you think you're doing?"

"What's it look like?"

"Like you're looking for trouble."

"No harm in listening," I said.

She shook her head. "But there is," she said softly and then she walked inside the club.

It was, in retrospect, foreshadowing. I was crazy to be there. But she was so beautiful that, if there was any way at all I thought she was right and it was time to go, I couldn't. Her skin was smooth and creamy, the color of toast, and her jet-black hair was shiny and pulled straight back from her face. She wore a pair of faded jeans and a ruby-colored peasant shirt that revealed her shoulder. I went back there every Friday night for four weeks and it wasn't until the fourth time that she got into my truck and we drove down River Road. It wasn't until weeks later that I said I loved her but, truly, I fell in love with her the moment I saw her. But you see, what people said was true: When you crossed that invisible line, you risked your life.

My mother was only eighteen when she gave birth to me. Hard to believe she was just a year older than I was when Laura and I fell in love. Sophie is twenty and there's still an innocence to her. I can't picture her with a baby, let alone a handful of a two-year-old boy.

My mother quit school in the eighth grade when her folks sent her to work on a tobacco farm. As the oldest of eleven kids, she was expected to help support the family and not to exceed the required schooling. She always told me how she worked from dawn until dusk, came home and ate dinner and then read. I believed her because when I was growing up, she always had her nose in a book. Her most cherished possession was her library card. She had it laminated in a machine at the old bus depot and she'd take two books out every week—one for me and one for her—and read while she was cooking and waiting for the wash to line-dry and while I was eating the snacks she made for me after school. She had this funny way of reading: She'd drag her index finger along the sentences and her lips moved. If she got to a funny part she'd smile, and if it was sad she'd say "aww" out loud. She was in another world when she was reading. She said she did all her traveling through books, more than she could ever do if she took the bus. Why, I've been to San Francisco and Paris and even London in the old days, she said.

The Christmas before I left town, I bought her a dictionary. Just a little paperback but she was so thrilled you would have thought it was a diamond necklace or something. Every night, she'd read through the dictionary, and then she'd shut it with a clap, open it with her eyes closed, and circle the opened page with her finger, landing on what she called her "word of the day" and then she'd use it in a sentence.

"Listen to this," she said one night. "Mellifluous. The way my son plays piano is mellifluous."

The last thing on my mind was leaving Warrensville without my mother. I dreamed that she and I would take the Trailways to Raleigh one night when Dad was at the bar drinking or during the day when he was at the paper mill. In Raleigh, we'd take the first train and ride it as far as it would go and then get on the next one and ride that one farther and just keep going until we got to, say, San Francisco. I figured Mama could get some kind of job and I would finish high school and then go on to college. Maybe Mama could even finish high school. We didn't need a fancy place. I had started saving my money for that day. I had eighty dollars stashed in the pocket of a shirt in the back of my closet, hidden really well so he wouldn't find it and turn it into drinking money. I'd worked at the gas station and valet parked at the catering hall and had enough for two bus tickets to someplace far enough away from him.

God, I hated him.

Just a few nights before I left Warrensville for good, Mama said she was sounding out words when he came in the door drunk as a skunk and told her to get him a beer. "Just one second, please, Luther," she said. It turned my stomach. She was always saying "please" and "thank you" and was just so kind to him. Now I realize she was probably just scared. Well, Luther said he didn't have to wait and then he snatched the dictionary from her hand and lit a match to it and held it and laughed while it went up in flames. She told me what happened when I came home and I promised to buy her another one. And there he was, passed out in his old armchair, and though I wanted to pull him up and shake him, there is no way that anyone can hit a passed out drunk, whether he deserves it or not. Especially when the man is your father.

I shook off the memories and checked into a small hotel on Main Street. It was clean and well-appointed and my room looked across Thunder River. I heard the falls in the distance. I lay a clean shirt on the bed, put my wallet and keys on the dresser, took off my clothes, and walked naked to the shower. It was my imagination but I felt like I could smell the river as the water cascaded over my shoulders. I wrapped a towel around my waist and lay down on the bed and wondered if it was possible to retrieve a lifetime.

CHAPTER NINE

Olivia

It's just over a three-hour drive from Willow to Chatham and rather dismal and desolate in spots until you cross the bridge and get on the narrow highway that leads to the Cape. In truth, the other side can be dreary as well, but never for me, because it leads me home. Even in November, the salt air is palliative, healing—as my father said his whole life, "for whatever ails you." I often wish the salt air had been more potent for his sake.

My parent's car, a ten-year-old model of the old Roadmaster that moved me from Manhattan, sat in the driveway, covered with a green tarpaulin. My father can no longer drive and my mother never did, yet my mother won't part with the car. Giving it up would be too final an act of resignation. Nina and I had encouraged our mother to drive. We'd tried to teach her, but as soon as she turned the key in the ignition, she would fret and argue that there was no need for her to learn since our father took her anywhere she needed to go. Now, Nina and I alternate turns taking her for a big shop every two weeks and the young couple, who recently moved next door, take her on errands when the visiting nurse comes for my father. Unfortunately, the nurse is really nothing more than a glorified baby-sitter. She bathes and grooms him—though he prefers my mother—and plays silly games that irritate him, although she maintains they stimulate his cognitive abilities. I am certain that he processes more than he is able to express and her games and grooming make him feel humiliated and infantilized. Sometimes I wish that his pain was physical, arthritis or even a heart condition, something that could be relieved or abated with medication. In his compromised mental state, we have little recourse, no miracles, no panaceas or analgesics. His mental demise was slow and deliberate, coinciding with or perhaps affecting his inability to do the physical tasks he once enjoyed and that came so easily. It was hard to tell whether his confusion forced him to become more sedentary and less courageous when it came to simple chores like gardening or home repairs, or whether he simply aged and lacked the physical strength. Nonetheless, his muscles atrophied and his physical and mental limitations became the proverbial vicious cycle. At first, we attributed his absentmindedness and confusion to depression. I still have not discounted that diagnosis, although the doctors maintain he suffers from Alzheimer's. I can't help but wonder, though, if his aging simply caused him to retreat to a world where memories of the past were less taxing than coping with the present as an old man.

I saw my mother peeking through the kitchen window as I pulled my Jeep up the driveway.

"Well, this is a treat," she said, opening the door and literally pulling me inside. She wore her signature baby-blue housecoat. She looked weary. I kissed her cheek and hugged her, startled by her frailty, thinking if I squeezed any harder, she might break.

"Are you eating? You're so thin, Mommy." She had no weight to lose to begin with.

She shrugged. "Henry hardly eats a thing."

"No, *you*," I said. "Are *you* eating?" Was there no place where she left off and Henry began?

"Come see you father," she said, avoiding the question. "Today's been a good day."

My father sat in a rocker on the sun porch, staring through the window at the Sound, a dark blue fleece covering his legs. He wore a plaid shirt and his gray hair fell long and stringy over the back of his collar.

"Daddy?" I called as I came toward him.

He turned his head to the side. "Who's that?"

"Olivia." I walked over to him and leaned over, kissed his cheek, then stood with my hands on his shoulders. "What do you see out there?"

"Some crazy guy's fishing. Sea's too big for fish today. Son of a bitch doesn't know what the hell he's doing."

My mother's face broke into a smile. "See? Good day," she whispered. "When he swears, I know he's feeling like himself." She poked him. "Tell her what we had for breakfast, Henry."

"Flapjacks."

"And, what else?"

"Jelly beans."

My mother's face fell. "Henry."

I stroked the back of his head. "You need a haircut. You look like a hippie."

"Your mother's a hippie. She's a communist."

I tried not to laugh. In her heyday, Margaret was far more liberal than Henry. Political discussions in our house always resulted in my father calling her a "pinko."

"So, Daddy, I'm staying over. I brought Emmet with me." I turned to my mother. "I don't have to teach on Monday so I might just stay through, OK?

"Who's Emmet?" my father asked.

"You know Emmet, Daddy. My dog. He's roaming around the yard."

"Well, bring him here and let's see him. Can he hunt?"

I laughed. "Hardly. Besides, you don't hunt."

"Dog's no good if he can't hunt." My father tapped his fingers on the arm of his rocker. "Where's that husband of yours? He called."

My face blanched. "He's out of town." I turned to my mother. "He called? From where?"

"Henry, now you know that no one called." My mother turned to me. "He's confused, Livi and what . . ."

She was about to say something else when my father clenched his fists and then splayed his fingers and clenched his fists again. "He's coming for dinner."

"Who's coming for dinner, Daddy?" I asked gently, patting my mother's arm to calm her. She hated when he raved.

"Noah," he said. "Nice boy, that Noah."

I placed a hand over my mouth and caught my breath. "I'm going to bring in my bag and get Emmet," I said.

My mother tucked the blanket around my father's legs and followed me to the door.

"Livi, I'm sorry."

"It's OK, Mommy," I said, thinking there was a deep beauty and peace somewhere in delusion.

"Livi, you said Carl had paperwork and you told Henry he's out of town," my mother said as we walked to the Jeep. "What's going on? Did you have an argument?"

"I don't know where he is," I said. "I was going to tell you." Tears rolled down my cheeks. It was the first time I allowed myself to cry since Carl left. "He left the house yesterday morning but he never went to campus. I haven't seen him since." I wiped my cheeks with my sleeve. "Damn it."

"For goodness sakes," she said. Her face was a bit pale. She was trying not to show alarm but not hiding it well.

"He left me a note. He won't say where he is but he says he's fine and he'll explain."

"Is there someone else?"

She surprised me. I didn't think my mother thought that way. "Why does everyone ask that?"

"Who's everyone?"

"Nina. The police."

"You called the police?"

"I called before I found the note. I felt I should. Just to be sure."

Just then my father bellowed from the sun porch. "Meg! Meg!"

My mother nearly ran. "Henry! Listen to you hollering like that! Now, what's the matter?"

He pointed toward the beach. "Son of a bitch caught one."

"Well, would you look at that?" she said patiently. "Maybe he'll catch another. You keep your eye on him, Henry. Olivia and I are going to make dinner now, Henry." She spoke the way one cajoles a child.

My father didn't answer. He just stared out the window.

We went to the kitchen and although I wanted Emmet to stay with my father, he followed the scent of the chopped meat that my mother pulled from the fridge. I scrubbed the Idaho potatoes while my mother mixed the meat in a bowl with oatmeal and ketchup and spices. I put the potatoes in a colander, wiped my hands on my jeans, and pulled Carl's letter from my pocket. I read it aloud.

"What do you think?" I asked.

"He's reassuring you," my mother said positively.

"Reassuring me? He leaves without a reason and you think this is comforting?"

"I just have a feeling he's gone to resolve something. It's like a mission."

I was thinking that she had become as dotty as my father. "A mission? Like what, the CIA?"

"Don't be ridiculous. I'm speaking personally.

"What are you talking about? You're not making any sense."

"We get to a point in life where we often need to purge

our souls, so to speak. You, too." She hesitated. "Let him go, Olivia."

"Let him go? I had no choice. He left . . ."

"I'm not talking about Carl. I'm talking about Noah. Let him go, Olivia," my mother said softly.

My voice trembled. "What makes you think I haven't let him go?"

"Because you're my daughter and I know you as well as I know myself."

I busied myself with setting the table. "Well, maybe you don't know yourself as well as you think—or me."

My mother smiled and put her arms around me. "Oh, yes, I do. I am eighty years old and believe me when I tell you that I know myself very well—and you."

"And I suppose you knew yourself well at fifty, didn't you?"

"Better than you do, my dear."

My eyebrows shot up. "Really? I think I'm insulted." I didn't want to fight with her.

"After dinner, after your father's settled, you and I should go through the attic."

"What for?"

"Cleansing."

It was knee-jerk reaction. "I don't want to."

"Oh, I know you don't want to."

"Why are you doing this? Why now? Maybe I'm going through enough right now."

"Olivia, there haven't been too many times that I steered you wrong."

"I don't see what this has to do with anything."

"Go get your father. The burgers are nearly ready." She hung her apron over a kitchen chair. "He'll protest, I warn you. He'll say he's not hungry. You'll have to coax him a bit."

"How?"

She sighed. Exasperated. "Same way you got Daniel to eat his green beans. You'll figure it out."

"How do you keep going? How can you bear to see him this way?"

"I can't. He breaks my heart," she said, biting her lower lip. "But once, a long time ago, he mended it."

CHAPTER TEN

Olivia

After dinner, I took my father to the den while my mother did the dishes. Had I not been there, she would have gone upstairs with my father and readied him for bed, leaving the dishes to soak overnight unless she managed to creep out without disturbing his slumber. The way that she, a slight, nearly frail, eighty-year-old woman, stayed awake after a day that required the physical strength of two people astounded me. That evening, my mother played the radio while she did the dishes. She was listening to Dick Golden, a Cape tradition, who broadcasts jazz six nights a week. When my father was well, she and my father used to dance together in the den. Nina and I often watched them surreptitiously and even though we were outwardly embarrassed as kids, in older years we remarked that the love they shared was enviable.

"So, what should we do, Dad?" I asked, sitting beside him on the worn sofa. "What do you say we look at pictures?"

My father looked at me blankly but I took several old photo albums from the shelf anyway. "Look, Daddy. Here's Nina, Frank, and Jillian."

My father nodded. "And here's your brother Alec. Where's Alec? He coming by?"

Alec had died five years before, but I didn't remind him.

"Oh, and here's your mother." My grandmother was in her thirties in the photograph, wearing a white dress and standing on the deck of a ship. "I wonder where she was off to."

"You look like her," he said suddenly. "You ever talk to her?"

What was the point? "Just yesterday," I said.

"She still up in Rockport?"

I nodded.

He swayed back and forth until he fell asleep. My mother tiptoed into the room.

"He's sleeping," I said. "What do we do?"

She prodded him a bit, placed a pillow behind his head, and asked me to help her swing his legs up on the couch. "He'll wake up again in an hour or two and then we'll get him upstairs."

I was incredulous. "How do you do this by yourself?"

"What choice do I have?"

"But you're always alone. I mean, even when he's not sleeping . . . "

"I turn on the television or the radio. I knit." She smiled. "I answer all his silly questions and sometimes I tell him a story. Then he drops off and I . . . " She searched for the ending to the sentence.

"You what?"

"I think." She cleared her throat. "I have *too* much time to think, actually. But I guess it's better than talking to myself, I suppose." She laughed. "Of course, I do that, too."

"We all do. What do you think about?"

"Oh, you and Nina. My grandchildren. Better times."

"I should spend more weekends with you."

"You have your own life, Livi."

"It doesn't matter."

"It does matter." She reached into a drawer and pulled out what looked like a walkie-talkie.

"What's that?"

"Baby monitor," she said, blushing. "I have the base over there on the bookshelf. I have one in every room, and when I leave him I carry the monitor around so I can hear him if he calls."

I sighed. "Oh, Mommy."

"Don't, Livi. I'm not one for pity. That's not going to change anything, " she said defiantly. "It'll make it worse."

"It's so unfair."

"That it is. But Aunt Harriet comes by, and the neighbors. Kind people." She clutched the monitor in her hand. "Come, now, we'll see if this works in the attic. You think you have the strength to yank down those stairs?"

"Do we really need to do this *now*?"

"No time like the present."

I groaned. "Oh, that was loaded."

"Read Carl's note to you again. I don't know what he's up to but I do know that sometimes we have to go back and put things to rest before we can move on."

"What makes you think I haven't moved on? I have children. I have a home and a husband."

A husband. I rarely used the sobriquet. Carl was Carl.

When I first met Carl, he was persistent. In the beginning, Carl came to the Cape nearly every weekend and stayed at the Chatham Bars Inn and, after dinner, I went home to my parents. It wasn't until we had known each other for six months that I spent the night with him. I remember that first morning when I came home the next day feeling like a skulking teenager. I went into the kitchen and my father nodded to me in disapproval, went to his den and slammed the door. When he left the room, my mother turned to me.

"Never mind him," she said. "So?"

"So? So, nothing."

"Are you OK?"

"Why wouldn't I be OK?" I didn't tell her that I cried after Carl and I made love that first time.

"It's all right, you know," she said. She waited for me to say something but I just poured my coffee and put a slice of bread in the toaster. "You're a grown woman."

My mother never ceases to amaze me. Sometimes I think that Daniel is more like her than either Carl or myself.

§

About a year and a half after we met, Carl took me to what is now our house. It was February. The Connecticut River was nearly frozen and the winding icy road leading to the house was treacherous. A handwritten FOR SALE sign was nailed to the porch, and because the trees were bare, the view of the valley was unobstructed and breathtaking.

"It needs work," Carl said. "I figure once the hedges are trimmed and the trees are cut back . . . and it needs a coat of paint."

"Are you thinking of buying it?"

"Maybe. It depends."

Until then, Carl lived in faculty housing at Belvedere, a one-bedroom apartment in what was once federal housing in a depressed section of Willow. The houses were dilapidated, flat-roofed structures that stood in what was once a middle-class neighborhood filled with families.

"Depends on what?"

"Come," he said and took me down to the dock. An old wooden rowboat was pulled halfway onto the shore, the other half sculpted in ice. He looked into the distance and shaded his eyes from the glare of the winter sun. "It's beautiful, isn't it?"

I nodded and he held me close to him. "I want us to live in this house, Olivia," Carl said, taking a blue velvet box from his pocket. He opened the lid and pulled out a small glistening diamond ring, holding it so that it caught the sunlight. I heard Noah's voice talking about children and moving to Cape Cod and then I heard sirens and saw him as they wheeled him through the electric doors of the emergency room. I gasped.

"Olivia?"

I looked up at Carl.

"I love you, Olivia," Carl said. "I've never loved anyone enough to want to spend my life with them. I want to marry you."

"Yes," I whispered, stretching out my hand to him, palm up. He took my hand and turned it over in his, and slipped the ring on my finger.

A breeze rustled the leaves and bent the bulrushes around the river bank.

"I want this to be forever," he said.

And I thought to myself that nothing ever is.

Yet I felt safe with Carl, a sense that frightened me enormously since feeling safe was too dangerous an emotion. It's a strange thing about visceral sensations. I felt a connection to Carl distinctly different from what I'd had with Noah. A nearly amorphous connection that found my heart and hand reaching out to him, afraid to grasp. Perhaps it was the separate yet common history we shared of weathering tragedy, resilience, and pain. There was something in Carl that I felt deep inside my soul.

We walked back to the empty house. The door was unlocked and he pushed it open. "So, what do you think?"

I put my arms around him and leaned my head into his chest. He was good and kind and tender. He was handsome and smart. He was willing to give me his damaged heart and take mine as well. I leaned into his chest and murmured, "I love you," words I never thought I would say to any other man, and tried desperately to shake the sense of betrayal.

We walked upstairs to what would be the master bedroom. There were French doors leading outside to a long balcony overlooking the river.

"Look at the view." he said, standing behind me, his arms around my waist.

I didn't tell him that those winding balconies were once known as widow's walks, narrow paths where women paced to and fro waiting for their men to return from the sea.

⑤

"Livi?" My mother's voice broke my thoughts. "You're in a trance."

"I am."

"Come, let's get going. I want to tell you a story."

I was expecting one of my mother's many parables, the feel-good tales she sometimes told to paint the world rose.

I groaned. "Well, maybe you can just give me the moral and skip the storytelling."

"Oh, now don't be so fresh," she said. "There's no moral to this one, really. Besides, this one is about me."

CHAPTER ELEVEN

Olivia

The Bessler stairs were stiff and creaky. I wasn't sure if I had the strength to yank them down, but when my mother stepped in to help, I mustered all the muscle I had for fear she'd dislocate her arm. They came down with a crash and we listened to the intercom for a moment, waiting to hear if the ruckus woke my father.

"That man always slept through everything," my mother said. "He claimed it was from the war days when they slept in the trenches."

"Everything was the war."

"But if I tiptoe from the room now, he stirs."

My mother walked up the stairs ahead of me, my hand poised behind her, although I pictured her misstepping and the two of us tumbling to the bottom. She is surprisingly spry for someone her age.

"You OK?" I asked.

"Fine," she said, pulling a handkerchief that was tucked into the sleeve of her shirt. She blotted her cheeks. "It's awfully dusty up here, isn't it?"

"Why couldn't you tell me the story downstairs?"

"Visual effects," she said with a smile.

Our attic is a museum. Every New Year, Nina and I promise to spend a day going through boxes of old school papers,

books, and toys, but somehow we never get around to it. There
are framed posters and paintings leaning against the walls, suitcases brittle with age, bed frames, carpet remnants, clothing
that has finally achieved vintage status.

"Here," my mother called from a corner on the far side.
"Over here."

There was a small metal file cabinet with a padlock. My
mother reached up and ran her hand along a wooden beam and
pulled down a key. "If this doesn't work, you run down and get
a bar of soap to wax the lock."

"Or a sledgehammer."

She placed the key into the lock and it turned. "Well, what
do you know?"

She lifted the lid, gingerly, anticipating, as though it were a
treasure chest. She took out an old yellowed envelope with
a circular stain that looked as if someone had once used it as a
coaster. Inside were several photographs wrapped in thin, tired
tissue paper. She looked through them, one by one, and a smile
crossed her face. "Here," she said, handing one to me.

It was a picture of a young man in uniform. I turned it over:
GEORGE NICKERSON 1941 BACK BAY was written in my mother's
script. "Who's this?"

"Once he was my heart," my mother said simply.

"Who is he?"

"Who *was* he," she corrected sadly. "George and I knew each
other from the time we were about ten years old. It was the old
story. He lived a few houses away and sat behind me in the
classroom. And, of course, he tortured me, which was a sure
sign that a boy liked you." She smiled. "Didn't quite dip my
pigtails in the inkwell but if there'd been one, he would have.
So, by the time we were both around fourteen, we had no doubt
that we were in love and, as soon as it was possible, we were
going to get married. But George was old-fashioned. He didn't
want to marry me until he had some money in the bank. After

high school, he went to night school for his CPA and worked days in an insurance office. I was going to stenography school. Then, Pearl Harbor was bombed and George enlisted, which was what every able-bodied boy did back in those days, and before he left, we got married. We were eighteen."

"Oh, my God. He was your *husband*. So then Daddy's your . . ."

"Second husband."

"Oh, my God."

"Oh, Livi, for goodness sake, stop."

To be perfectly honest, suddenly my mother's sexuality became a reality. Marrying my father was one thing. Marrying another man was another.

"Don't look so shocked," she said.

"Why didn't you ever say anything?"

"There was no reason to."

"So, why now?"

"Well, if you'd stop talking and listen."

"OK," I said obediently.

"Now, where was I? Oh, yes, so we got married. Lots of people needed money back in those days and rented out space for a song. We took a room on the third floor of someone's home. The landlord gave us hours when we could use the kitchen." My mother sighed. "So, George and I lived in that room for three months and they were the best three months of my life." My mother looked nearly dreamy. "We pretended peas were caviar and soda pop was champagne. We spent hours talking and listening to the radio and dancing. And then the day came when George shipped out. It was December and I went down to the dock with the other military wives and we all were wearing white gloves and waving good-bye. It was freezing and all the women were crying and I remember thinking that the tears were going to freeze on our cheeks. Somewhere deep inside, I knew that George wouldn't come home. About a month after he left, I missed and, sure enough, I was pregnant. I wrote to

George but I never heard back. I doubt he even got the letter. Five months later, in May, I got the telegram that George was killed. He was on the carrier Yorktown and it was hit through the flight deck and George was on the flight deck at the time. Two days after I got the news, I miscarried. I lost George and his baby within days of one another. George came home a few weeks later in a pine box and I buried him next to our son, George Robert Nickerson, Jr."

"Oh, Mommy."

My mother took a deep breath. "They're both in Dorchester. Pine Hills. In the beginning, I went to see them all the time. The last time was just after your father and I got engaged. I went back to tell George. I suppose in reality I was talking to myself but I felt he could hear me. I told him I was going to marry your father."

"Did you love Daddy?" I whispered.

"Why, of course, or I wouldn't have married him, for goodness sake." She seemed almost indignant.

"You met Daddy when you worked at the hospital, right?"

"I was volunteering and that's when I decided to go to nursing school. I needed to take care of people since I felt I wasn't doing a great job caring for myself. I wanted to help the boys who had made it home. I also needed to make a living. Your father had served his tour and spent time there counseling the fellows who were casualties. A lot of the vets did that back then. Moral support. We had psychiatrists and doctors but talking to someone who'd been there was important. Now, your father *knew* George. Not very well because George was younger than your father but your father had gone to school with George's older brother. Rockport was an even smaller town back then."

I looked at George's picture. "He was very handsome."

"And kind, and hard working. He made me laugh more than anyone, and then when he died he made me cry more tears than I ever thought I had. He was my life. He was my child-hood." She looked up at me. "He was my best friend."

"And Daddy was OK with that?"

"He was. And the more I told him about George and the more he listened without a jealous bone in his body, the more I came to love your father. Livi, after George was killed, I didn't think I would ever fall in love again."

"And you didn't feel like, I don't know, that you were be-traying George when you fell in love with Daddy?"

"Oh, I did. At first. But then I felt grateful. If I had been the one to die, I would have wanted George to fall in love and live a happy life."

"I wish you had told me all this before."

"You were a child."

"I haven't been a child for quite a while," I said softly.

"Well, I suppose that part of me felt it was too personal. No one would have understood. The love I felt for your father was an entirely different love than the one I had with George." My mother's eyes were distant. "With George, everything was new and hopeful, and we were filled with dreams. When I met your father, I was as badly wounded as those soldiers in the hospital. I might as well have lost an arm or a leg or been paralyzed. When I met your father, I had no more illusions or romantic no-tions. I knew that fate wasn't discriminating when it came to love."

"So, you didn't feel guilty or disloyal when you fell in love with Daddy?" I asked.

She laughed. "He wasn't 'Daddy' when I met him. He was Henry Hughes and I tried with all my might not to love him." She paused. "Of course, I felt guilty at first. And I was afraid to let myself love someone again, because what if I lost them? But I married Henry and buried George. More, I put George to rest. When I was at George's grave, telling him about your father, a woman came up the path and stopped at a grave about three rows away from George. She put a small wreath at the base and kneeled down and touched her fingers to her lips and then to the stone. After she left, I looked at the inscription. She looked to be in her forties. I wanted to see who she was mourning. There were so many grieving women in those days. The headstone said Clarence Knowles and that he was born in 1898 and died in 1918 which told me that he was probably killed in the First World War."

"I can't believe you remember all that."

"It was important to me," she said shyly. "I figured the deceased was either her brother or her husband. I watched her walk up the path and there was a man waiting for her. She kissed his cheek and they walked off, hand in hand. I tried to catch up to her."

"What for?"

"I wanted to know who was buried there. What he meant to her."

"What difference did it make?"

"Because when she kissed that other man on the cheek, her face lit up. If Clarence had been her beau or her husband, I thought maybe there was hope for me."

"Did you ever find out?"

"No, but it was better that way because I decided to think of her as my future. I thought, here I am in my twenties and I'm falling in love with Henry and if I don't stop fretting and feeling scared and guilty and all those things, I'll wind up in my forties and alone. I liked to think that the woman had fallen in love again, too, and was coming to visit the grave of someone who was still in her heart. Hearts are big enough for more than one person, Olivia. We learn that when we have children, now, don't we? We love the first child more than we can ever imagine and then love the second just as much, but differently. Those chambers in the heart have plenty of room in them for everyone."

"So, you never went back to George's grave after that?" I dropped my voice. "Or the baby's?"

She shook her head. "Partially, I suppose, it's been geography. I've been here in Chatham since your father and I married in 1945. Lord knows, I don't get off this Cape too often. And I would never have felt right asking Henry to take me to visit George. It would have been asking too much."

"Have you wanted to?"

"Oh, yes. Especially after you were born. I felt like I should tell George about you. You know, I was always convinced that I didn't conceive you as quickly as I conceived my first baby because it wasn't time. I think it was nature's way of making sure I was settled and ready for a baby again."

"Were you afraid that you'd miscarry with me?"

"Yes and no. As a nurse, I felt that I lost that baby because of the trauma I suffered. I didn't think it was anything physiological."

"Mommy, I can take you to Dorchester, you know."

"Well, let's make a deal. We'll go visit George and then we'll visit Noah."

My heart stopped.

"You've never been to his grave, have you?" she asked.

I shook my head. "I can't."

"You can." She closed the metal box and put George's picture back inside.

I was uncomfortable. "What for? What would be the purpose? It was so long ago."

My mother looked through me in the dim attic light. "Let's go see your trunk in the corner."

I began to protest.

"Memory keeps us truly alive. Look at your father. Look how devastating it is for all of us that he doesn't remember. I remember your father when he was young and strong and vital. When he was my safe harbor. Now he looks at me and half the time he doesn't even know who I am. Part of me vanished within him."

"That's not true. He calls for you. He panics when you leave the room."

"That's instinct. Not much more than when Emmet follows you around the house," my mother said adamantly. "Sometimes your father thinks I'm his mother or his Aunt Lil. And even when he calls my name it's not because I'm his wife—it's habit."

"Well, maybe losing our memory can also be salvation."

"Certainly not for those around us. And even with your father, sometimes I wonder how much he's lost and how much of it is an inability to process, and express himself."

"I'm surprised you didn't tell me about George after Noah died."

"Oh, I thought about it. On one hand, I didn't want to steal your thunder. It was your time to mourn."

"And the other?"

"It was history repeating itself. Your pain was so close to my heart. You're my daughter and once I felt precisely the way you were suffering. I felt your pain so deeply."

"You could have told me when I met Carl."

"You were closed off. I didn't think you'd be receptive. What was that expression you kids said back then? It wasn't where your head was at?"

I laughed. "Fortunately, we don't say that anymore." I thought for a moment. "I wanted to marry Carl but part of me felt like I still hadn't left Noah—like I was still his wife. Does that make sense?"

"You *still* haven't left Noah."

"That's not true!"

"I think it is. A long time ago you said you would never love anyone the way you loved Noah. Do you remember what I told you?"

"Not exactly."

"I said it wouldn't be the same, but that didn't mean you wouldn't love someone else."

"That was twenty-five years ago. How can you think I'm not past all that?"

"I wasn't always an old woman, Olivia. I wasn't always your mother. And when I married your father my heart still wasn't entirely healed. It still isn't. Don't think for a moment that I look at George's picture and don't feel a pang. Your pangs are still on the surface. You still haven't let go."

I looked in her eyes. They were steel blue. She was still beautiful. "This is the old joke, isn't it? When the child says the parent is much smarter than she used to be."

She ignored my compliment. "There's a fatalism to life. If George hadn't died, I wouldn't have met your father and I wouldn't have you and Nina. It's just not always a smooth road. No one warns you about the detours."

"But if George hadn't died, you would have had *George's* babies."

"But I *didn't*," she said emphatically.

I could no longer resist. "So, where's my trunk?"

She pointed to the other side of the attic. "Exactly where you left it."

"This is like an exorcism."

She shook her head. "There are no bad spirits."

"A séance then."

"No," she said firmly. "We're not trying to raise the dead." She took my chin in her hand. "We're trying to settle the living."

I couldn't refuse my mother. She was a woman as vulnerable as myself. Until then, I had only known half-truths about my mother and acknowledged only half-truths about myself. It was time to unearth my secrets.

CHAPTER TWELVE

Carl

It was around five o'clock in the morning and pitch black outside the window when I awoke in Warrensville that first morning. My sleep had been fitful. I dreamed of the house I lived in as a boy: I was leaning against my mama's old oak chifforobe, reading aloud to her from *A Wrinkle in Time* while Mama ironed my school clothes. Funny that was the book I was reading in my dreams since time is wrinkled so severely now. In the dream, mirrors kept breaking around me each time I caught my reflection, and I sat in piles of shattered glass.

My stomach growled and my head pounded. All I wanted was a cup of hot coffee. I took two aspirins from a small vial I always carry in my pocket and hoped it would do the trick until I could get myself some breakfast. I lay back on the bed, a cool cloth across my forehead, and waited for the throbbing to lift. I thought back to The First Baptist Church on Market Street where Mama took me every Sunday. She'd get all dolled up in her "going-to-meeting" clothes and dress me in gray cotton trousers, a white shirt with a red bow tie, and a navy blazer. I wore those same clothes two years in a row until the pants got so short they hung above my socks and the sleeves on the blazer pulled so tight under my arms that one day they finally ripped. My mother had two church dresses. One was lavender with small white polka dots and the other was black, just in case there was a member of the parish who had died and she needed to pay her respects.

When the day came that I needed new "meeting" clothes, Mama and I went to the One More Time shop and bought some second-hand but new-to-me slacks and shirt and blazer. She spied a yellow dress with a big wide belt made of patent leather. I was eight years old. She was twenty-six. So young it's hard to fathom. I waited outside the curtain of the makeshift dressing room. She came out and twirled in front of me.

"So, what do you think, sweet pea? It's five dollars and I suppose I don't really need it, but it's just so nice."

I said she looked real pretty and then the shop lady came over and said she looked like someone should take her picture for the cover of one of those fashion magazines they sell at the drugstore. Had I been older, I might have told her that my father drank up more than five dollars at the bar every night and she should just buy the damn dress and let him forego a few drinks.

I swung my legs over the side of the bed and made my way to the sink where I threw cold water on my face and brushed my teeth, ran a wet comb through my hair, got dressed, and went downstairs. The clerk was dozing behind the desk, a tattered cardigan buttoned to the neck and a scarf on top of that. It was so cold in Warrensville the night before that my car was etched in feathers of frost. I remembered passing a Texaco station on my way into town and figured I'd get a cup of coffee and one of those cellophane-wrapped danishes.

I drove out River Road, lost in thought, when I realized that I had passed the turn for the Texaco. Instead, I was headed in the direction of Holy Mount. It must have been about six-thirty now and the sun was just beginning to rise, purple and orange and still low in the sky. I made a left turn into the iron gates and parked the car at a curb. I walked the rows of headstones and knew exactly where I was headed as if it were yesterday. There were statues of seraphs and angels everywhere I turned. Elaborate homage to the dead. Wreaths and flowers were wilted by the unseasonable frost. I spied the familiar spot ahead where the morning sunlight fell in a patch of gold by the weeping willow tree. I stood before the grave.

Carl Larkin
Born January 10, 1901
Died August 11, 1964
Beloved husband, father, teacher, friend

In so many ways, the grave is mine as well, not merely the grave of a man whose name I borrowed and never returned.

One choice, one quickly-made decision can change a life forever if it's the wrong one. Olivia's first husband walked into a liquor store at the wrong moment and was gone the next. Had he come in just a few minutes later he would have changed the course of three lives: his, Olivia's, and mine. Had I not seen Laura outside The Factory and fallen in love with her, none of this would have happened. But then again, I was what people called "trouble waiting to happen." It wasn't that I did things that were criminal, it was more that I seemed to have a penchant for being in the wrong place at the wrong time—whether it was Seaside or outside the schoolyard. When the beer cans were tossed into the woods, I seemed to be in the unfortunate position of being the one left holding the bag. I didn't run from the law but as my father's son, I was already a marked young man and, I admit, was often too quick with my fists—usually vindicating someone or something but nevertheless doing it in a way that never worked to my benefit. The one thing that saved me were my grades and my music. Straight A's—because I was determined and hellbent to get out of Warrensville and make something of myself. No way was I going to end up drinking after working all day at the paper mill.

My children are the continuation of me. Sophie plays music. Mostly violin, but the piano as well. There is a baby grand in our living room yet I have never touched the keys; once, music was my passion. I have told Sophie about the role of physics in music. How sound is nothing more than a wave created by vibrating objects propagated through a medium from one place to another. Beats and frequencies and the formula for the speed of sound, but I have never told her that I once sang in the church choir and played the piano at the preacher's house every day after school. In the house where I grew up, we barely had room for a divan in our living room, let alone a piano. I have seen Daniel's fists fly and heard the passion of his words when he felt he needed to right a wrong but I have never told him that his is the same spirit as mine—the one that drove me to leave Warrensville that steamy August night when I was seventeen. I never told him that he sends me soaring back to places where once I had the courage to go. He has no idea how deeply I feel his passion and the fire burning in his soul. I tried to mold science into my armor, hiding behind a series of disconnected ideas in the hopes that they will crystallize into something useful. I've tried to fool myself into believing I can erect a barrier that distances me from those I love or want to love. I can't.

Carl Larkin was my mentor, my teacher, my friend. He taught American Literature. It wasn't my best subject. He said that my essays overanalyzed and read too much symbolism into things that weren't there, yet he let me ramble on. I stayed after school just about every day to talk with him. Well, to listen to him speak. We talked about books mostly—books captured me the way they captured Mama and, although I often spoke to him in abstractions, somehow he knew what I was trying to say, reading between my lines. He comforted me. He gave me hope. And then, one night, he died in his sleep from a heart attack. It was just about six months before I left Warrensville. When I got out to Kansas and needed a new name, I took his. I wanted his. He seemed anonymous enough—widowed years before, two grown sons, both full-time military, one stationed somewhere in California and the other in Japan. When Dr. Larkin passed on, there were no Larkins left in Warrensville.

I stared at his grave and wondered whose name will be on mine when I am gone. I wondered if anyone would etch "beloved" on my headstone when the wind came for me.

CHAPTER THIRTEEN

Olivia

When I was around ten, I watched our neighbor's daughter, Linda, from my bedroom window as she went out on a Saturday night. She was about seventeen at the time. She wore tight skirts and tight sweaters and sometimes I'd see her light a cigarette inside the cab of her boyfriend's old Ford pickup. Her hair was long and thick and silky-smooth and her skin was clear and freshly made-up. I guessed she smelled like Charlie or Ambush and probably shaved her legs. I wanted to be grown up like Linda and it seemed an eternity away.

Adults always cautioned not to be impatient, whether it was about waiting to grow up or Christmas or summer vacation, all things that I anticipated with such urgency that my stomach churned. My father always said that things were "just around the corner" and would "come and go" before I knew it.

Of course, eighteen did come before I knew it, at least it seems that way looking back. There I was, the legal definition of grown-up, emancipated if I dared to be—and nothing momentous happened. Nothing felt different or changed. I went to college and instead of being heady with independence, I was homesick—until I met Noah in my sophomore year, and then home was with him.

I'd had crushes on boys in junior high and high school and spent endless hours with my girlfriends trying to decide if I was a Paul girl or a George girl but I had never been truly in love. Noah was the first boy who kissed me other than Kevin Malone, who took me to the senior prom, and that wasn't the same kind of kiss as Noah's. I didn't even want Kevin to kiss me. Noah was the first man I slept with and, as far as I was concerned, he would be the last. Noah was the promise of romance and a life that would be perfect. He was my fairytale.

🌀

When my mother and I opened the trunk, the calico was as bright and fresh as the day she glued it down and I swore it smelled like chlorine bleach. As I undid the latch, I didn't know what to expect, fearing the unthinkable would jump at me, seize me like Medusa's snakes and condemn me to a pain that had, until that moment, been effectively sequestered. Perhaps it was that youth is more courageous. At twenty-five, I surely had a greater sense of immortality despite Noah's loss than I have at fifty. Thinking back, I even had the strength to return to our apartment and gather what was left of my life, yet opening the trunk twenty-five years later was nearly terrifying.

My mother sat beside me on an old suitcase turned on its side as I read through letters that Noah and I wrote to one another over the course of our marriage. Peripherally, I saw her watching me, much like she had that summer. She let me weep without laying a hand on my back or offering any words of wisdom or comfort. This time I was on my own, although she took a clean folded handkerchief, embroidered with violets, from her cuff and put it in my hand.

I shook the snowglobes and watched the glittering confetti burst into a storm and rubbed my fingers along the enamel of the spoons. I looked at wedding pictures and silly posed shots we took with the camera perched precariously as one of us darted into the photograph. Noah looked exactly the way I remembered him yet my own youth astonished me.

The windmill was the last memory I opened. Folded in tissue, I peeled back the layers like an onion, waiting to get to the heart, stopping before it was completely exposed.

"Why am doing this? It won't bring him back," I said.

"That's not the purpose," my mother answered.

An anger welled inside me, misdirected at her. "This has no purpose! Why are you making me do this?" Tears stung my cheeks.

"Because it's time."

"I buried him."

"Burying the dead is overrated. They still don't leave us."

"When was the last time you looked at George's picture until today?"

My mother looked uncomfortable. "Last year. When your father got sick. But time to time over the years."

"Why?"

She thought for a moment. "Because he was part of me. Because your father doesn't remember anything about me, so I need to remind myself."

"I'm sorry. I'm not angry at you."

We mothers are a sorry lot. No matter what we do or don't do, our children find fault with us. We either do something too soon or not soon enough.

My mother nodded. "I know. You're just angry. I'm angry at your father. This is the time in life that we need companionship above all else and your father . . ." She shut her eyes for a moment. "I was angry at George for being on that flight deck, and at every woman whose husband or fiancé came home when mine didn't." She took me by the shoulders. "You were never *angry* when Noah was killed."

I felt like I couldn't breathe. "How could I be? He didn't do anything wrong. It wasn't his fault."

"It has nothing to do with *fault*. It's not your father's fault that he's the way he is now. It wasn't George's fault that he was killed." My mother hesitated. "Why weren't you angry at Noah's killer?"

"Because he was just a kid."

"So what? Does that excuse him from knowing right from wrong? From taking a life?"

I blocked my ears. "Stop!"

"Livi, you're not being honest. Not with yourself, not with your husband, not with me."

"Noah's not here anymore."

"Not Noah. Carl. *He's* your husband, Olivia."

I froze. "Oh, God," I whispered.

"Don't you believe he wouldn't have wanted happiness for you?"

I unwrapped the windmill and held it in my hand. "He was the sweetest boy. The kindest soul." I looked up at my mother. "I'll never understand why he was killed. What we did to deserve it."

"Not every question has an answer. Listen to me, Livi. Find a corner of your heart for Noah."

"And tuck him away? Just like that?"

"I told you before, there's plenty of room in there for everyone."

"We never said good-bye."

"Say good-bye now, Livi."

"Since when do you believe in things so, I don't know, so spiritual?"

"It's more dependable when you get older."

Just then the intercom crackled and my father's voice called, "Meg! Jesus, Meg! What the hell? Meg! Goddamn it!"

I started for the steps.

My mother stopped me and lowered the volume on the monitor.

"I'll go."

"What's wrong with him?"

"Nothing, really. He's disoriented when he first wakes up."
She sighed. "He's disoriented when he's falling asleep. Help me
down the stairs."

I heard her steps through the monitor as she made her way
to the bedroom, calling, "Coming, Henry."

I went back in the attic and shut the lid of the trunk. I took
the windmill, though. I listened to my mother's voice. *How
about some nice warm cocoa?* she asked my father. *Now, let's wash
your face a bit and get you back in bed.*

She was washing my father's face with a cloth when I came
into her bedroom. "Can I do anything?"

"We're fine. Right, Henry? Everything's fine." She folded the
cloth, placed it on the nightstand, and turned to me. "After I get
him settled, let's have some tea and amaretto. Go and boil the
water. I'll just be a few minutes."

I kissed my father's forehead. At that moment I realized that
the woman washing her husband's face with a cloth, and calming him just shy of a lullaby, never got to say good-bye to either
of her husbands.

CHAPTER FOURTEEN

Olivia

Nina showed up in Chatham on Sunday morning at nine o'clock. My parents were resting upstairs. My father had gotten up at five, made his way down to the kitchen, pulled every box of cereal from the cabinet, and shaken them onto the floor. I had just finished sweeping when Nina came through the back door.

I dropped the broom and ran to her. "This is the best surprise!"

"What happened here?"

"Dad," I said, knowing it didn't require further explanation. "She's upstairs—calming him down."

"It's bad, huh?"

"He has moments when he appears lucid and then he makes no sense at all. Doesn't know who anyone is, where he is. I think this cereal thing was frustration." I sighed. "It's gotten worse."

"Worse for her, too."

Nina held open the trash can while I emptied the dustpan. "Any news?"

I shook my head. "Nothing. I left my cell on all night and checked the answering machine a few minutes ago for the hundredth time. Nothing."

"Are you going to call the police again?"

"I don't know what to do."

"Did you say anything to the kids?"

"No," I said emphatically. "I spoke to Sophie yesterday. She knows I'm here. Daniel's a problem. He usually calls on Sunday nights, but I'm going to call him this afternoon and head him off at the pass." I laughed. "I sound like Dad. I'll spend the night here and head back early Tuesday morning. I don't have a class until the afternoon."

"Well, Frank's with Jillian and he can drop her at school tomorrow so I'll stay the night, too." She grinned. "Sleepover."

My mother padded down the stairs. "Well, thank goodness. I thought I was hearing voices!" She hugged Nina. "This is wonderful. Where are Jillian and Frank? You must have left at four in the morning!"

"Six. And they're home. I told them this was ladies only," Nina said with a grin. "Of course Jillian took some convincing that she wasn't a lady yet. So, now, what have you two been up to?"

My mother smiled. "Oh, not too much."

Nina looked back and forth between my mother and me. "What's funny?"

"She's a taskmaster," I said. "We went through the attic. All my old stuff."

"It must have been some night."

"Oh, it was," I said.

"Well, tomorrow we're going to draw straws for who gets to stay home with Dad and who takes Mommy to the hair salon," Nina said.

"Hair salon? Now, don't be ridiculous," my mother protested. "I haven't gone to the salon in months. I'll just wash my hair and that'll do just fine."

Nina and I shook our heads in unison. "Oh no," we said at once.

"Why, I guess you two think I look a fright." My mother looked hurt.

"It's scaring me," Nina teased.

"Nina!" I laughed and turned to my mother. "Pay no attention to her. She's always had a sick sense of humor. You're fine but you should get a rinse and a set and a little pampering." I cocked my head toward Nina. "*That's* what the ambassador meant to say."

"OK, so rock-paper-scissors for who gets to take Mommy and who stays with Dad," Nina said.

"You do realize you're having a severe regression, don't you?" I asked, laughing.

Nina inhaled through her nose and smiled. "My childhood comes back to me when I'm here."

"Well, I'm pleased to see it makes you feel silly and happy, " my mother said, smiling. "As for tomorrow, the nurse comes so we all have a reprieve." My mother looked down at her hands, so rough and chapped. "Terrible thing. Looking at time away from Henry as a reprieve."

"Hair, nails, pedicures. Total makeovers!" Nina said, purposely not addressing my mother's remark. Nina was always good at picking up everyone's pieces.

My mother giggled like a girl and then her eyes filled with tears. "It doesn't get better than this now, does it?" she said.

We all knew, of course, that it does but this was the best we could do for now.

I called Daniel that afternoon. He was with friends so he wasn't up for conversation. The fact that I was in Chatham with Nina and my parents pleased him. Daniel has a warm sense of family. The fact that Carl wasn't with me was acceptable since I used Nina's ladies-only excuse. We were giving Grandma a pick-me-up, I said with enough enthusiasm that Daniel didn't put me through his typical inquisition. I knew Daniel wouldn't call Carl. Unless Daniel had something specific to tell his father, there were no casual conversations. Still, I could see that both Carl and Daniel were reaching out a bit more, but neither was easy to reel in.

I called Willow at least a dozen times that afternoon and evening, and still no messages. I even called the Willow police, still uncertain that Carl was fine despite the reassurance of his note. Nina was by my side when the police said they had no information although enough time had elapsed if I wanted to file a missing person's report. Of course, Carl wasn't so much missing as I didn't know where he was.

"No news is good news, right?" I said as I hung up the phone. And for a second I swear that Nina and I shared a moment we had twenty-five years before when news had been horrendous.

"If Frank did this, I'd be beside myself," Nina said. "He has a lot of nerve putting you through this."

"He'll call," I said, quietly defending him. "He will."

That night, after our parents went to bed, Nina and I poured glasses of red wine and sat toe to toe on the window sill on the sun porch.

"Remember that summer? We sat here all the time," I said, staring at the beacon across the harbor. "I can't believe I survived."

"To youth," Nina said, raising her glass. "So, whose idea was it to go through the attic?"

"*Margaret's,*" I said, with a laugh. "I was a fly in her web."

Nina laughed. "How was it, really?"

I thought for a moment. "At first it felt like an unnecessary cruelty but then it was like watching dust settle particle by particle. I can't explain it. Like finally putting things away. Ultimately? I think it was good."

"I can't believe she got you to do it."

"Why?"

"Honestly? Because you never talk about anything. You're rather resistant."

"Am I?" I was surprised. "Well, she's pretty tough to resist. She may be little but she packs a wallop."

Nina smiled and sipped her wine. "She always did. He always acted like the one to wear the so-called pants in the family, but it was her."

I smiled. "He was louder."

"Yeah, but he was always a softie." Nina ran her finger along the rim of her glass. "When Noah died, he said it was like losing a son."

I thought of my father in younger, better days when his hands smelled like roses and he fished in the cove. "When I got here yesterday, Dad was confused and said that Noah called."

"Oh, no. What did you say?"

"Nothing. Mommy felt terrible. His mind is so addled. He's way back in the past."

Just then, my cell phone signaled a message. "I never even heard it ring, did you?" I punched in my voice mail code.

Olivia, it's me. Tried the house and I'm thinking you're at your folks but it's too late to call. I'm OK. I'll try you again tomorrow. I saved the message. "It was Carl."

"Call his cell phone," Nina said.

"He doesn't have one."

"What? Everyone has a cell phone. I saw a homeless guy talking on a cell phone the other day."

I laughed. "Carl is a technophobe. Listen." I replayed the message for her.

"Where is he?"

I shook my head. "I don't know." I scrolled through the call history. "Unavailable number, it says."

"And you're not worried."

"That's not true."

"I'd be out of my mind."

"The night Noah was killed, I heard the sirens and I just knew that something happened. I didn't know the extent of it, but something just told me he wasn't all right. I know Carl is alive." I looked in my sister's eyes. "My orientation is entirely different from yours."

"With good reason," Nina said gently.

"He sounds tired, though. Or something."

"Like what?"

"You know how you feel when you finally finish something and it's been a long haul but there's that feeling of finally being done? I used to feel that way when I finally got the kids to bed and I could sleep. That's how he sounds. Relieved in a way but you also know you have to get up again in a few hours."

I had enormous difficulty falling asleep that night. I once believed my relationship with Carl existed in diametric opposition and suddenly I questioned whether or not it was more a symbiosis. I was tormented, trying to decide if Carl and I were more kindred spirits than either of us dared to acknowledge. On the most primal level, I questioned why darkness was the only realm where we could make love. Why neither of us confessed that daylight might force revelations we preferred to conceal. I realized that in order to know another human being, to read an emotion and nuance in a voice, you have to have a knowledge of yourself. You have to accept yourself before you can accept someone else. This isn't to say the time in the attic with my mother resulted in a facile epiphany—it was simply that the evening with her, spent among memories, begged questions and coaxed answers.

My mother's confession humbled me. It gave me permission to love two men in my lifetime, validated by her ability to do the same. There comes a time when we become experts on our parents if they let us in, and then, if we're lucky, experts on our ourselves.

I never knew my father's parents, since they died when I

was too young to have the recall, but I remember my mother's. I always attributed my mother's stoicism and stiff upper lip to her parents. My grandfather was a veteran of the first World War and my grandmother had survived the famine in the Ukraine when she was in her late twenties. She'd emigrated to the United States against all odds of getting out of Russia and met my grandfather at a men's rooming house in Boston where she waited tables. Adversity was de rigueur for them. Of course, I had no idea when I lost Noah that my mother's determination for my life to go on was not attributable to stoicism as much as it was to losing George and their baby.

I wondered how we would fare and what we would change if we held the Promethean ability to see our futures. Would I have taken those five years with Noah anyway knowing that was all the time we would have together? Prometheus, of course, was bound to a rock for eternity.

🌀

It was four in the morning when I finally gave up on sleep, took my cell phone and went down to the kitchen. My mother was sitting at the kitchen table, a cup of chamomile tea cooling in front of her.

"What are you doing up?" we asked at the same time.

"The water's just boiled if you want tea," she said, not answering my question.

"I can't sleep." I played Carl's message for her. "I don't understand. Where is he?"

"Maybe nowhere," she said simply. My mother had become nearly mystical.

"Strange that you said that. When I first met Carl and asked where he preferred, Kansas or the South, he said Nowhere."

"Maybe he just needed to get away. To reflect."

I rolled my eyes. "He's hardly Thoreau. Did Daddy ever do anything like that?"

"Oh, no. He's much too practical for that sort of thing."

"Carl is practical."

"Apparently he's not as practical as you think. Certainly he's proven himself to be unpredictable. Your father was always a rat in a maze."

"If this is supposed to make me feel better, it's not."

"You can't write me a script, my dear."

"Well, *you're* practical. Have you ever done anything like this? Just taken off to think back?"

"I couldn't. I had children." She smiled.

I laughed. "Sorry we cramped your style."

"That's not what I meant."

"I know."

"I got away differently. Like last night in the attic."

"That's not the same."

"It's all just a question of venue." She sighed. "Do you know what Jillian said last night? She said that she couldn't wait for Thanksgiving break because homework sucks. Forgive me for this, Livi, but between your husband and mine right now, this all just sucks, doesn't it?"

The expression coming from my mother was too much. We laughed until our sides ached and tears rolled down our cheeks. We took our tea into the living room and watched infomercials for an hour. Guaranteed ways to get rid of wrinkles, cellulite, midriff bulges, bald spots, and acne.

"You think any of those things really work?" I asked.

She didn't answer and clicked the remote to The Weather Channel. She stared at the television as the screen changed forecasts from city to city.

"I want to go to Italy," she said out of the blue.

"You do?"

"Which part of Italy?" I asked.

"All up and down," she said, her voice resonating with defiance. "Just stomp all over the damn boot."

CHAPTER FIFTEEN

Olivia

Nina and I took our mother into town the next day. Her hair was rinsed and looked softer, the gray shinier. She had her toes polished in a pale pink (at our insistence) but refused to have any color on her fingernails since her hands were in water all day. We had lunch at The Squire, picked up some groceries, and bought two fuschia cyclamen plants for Mommy despite her protests that she had little time to care for plants. We convinced her that the cyclamen did best with benign neglect.

When we were kids, Nina and I watched *Queen for a Day*, and although my mother was usually busying herself about the house, when the chosen queen was draped in the fake ermine robe and crowned with the tiara, my mother always stopped what she was doing to watch. Of course, the prizes in those days were "female" things like refrigerators and freezers.

"I feel like that queen for a day," my mother said as we drove home. She looked at her nails. "Sure beats an Amana, though."

The nurse already had on her coat when we walked in the door—and was holding an ice pack on her hand. My father had been difficult, refusing to eat lunch (even though my mother prepared it before she left and it was the same soup and sandwich he had every day). He was disheveled, his shirt hanging over his sweat pants that had a dark circular spot on the front.

"What happened to your hand?" I asked the nurse.

"He hit me again." She turned to my mother. "Mrs. Hughes, I'm terribly sorry but I just can't come here anymore." She dropped the ice pack in the sink and gathered her bag. "No one's going to stay here with him. He's impossible."

My mother ignored the nurse and went to my father who had gone to sit in his rocker. He was looking out over the Sound.

"Let's get you changed now, Henry. Come with me," she said, placing her arm around his shoulders.

"Peed in my pants," he said gruffly. "Where have you been?"

"With the girls. Just in town."

"Don't do that again," he warned, with the same commanding intonation he had when he was younger.

"I won't, Henry," she said and kissed his cheek.

"Meg?"

"Yes?"

He took her hand and pressed it to his lips.

"This is why I could never go to Italy," my mother said without looking at Nina or me.

But, of course, we already knew that.

It wasn't easy to leave my parents on Tuesday morning. I waited until the last possible moment until it got to the point that I'd miss my class if there was any traffic at all once I got off the Cape. Nina left the night before which made it all the harder. My father stood on the porch with my mother as I warmed up the car.

"Where are you going?" he asked.

"Home. To Willow, Daddy. I'll be back soon."

"Over the bridge?"

"Over the bridge," I said, grateful to hear a trace of him.

"Crap," he said. "It's a load of crap."

I kissed my father good-bye and he waited obediently while my mother walked me to the car.

"You have your windmill?" my mother asked.

"In my bag," I said, patting the side of my purse.

"You let me know as soon as you hear from Carl. And take care—it's raining. The roads can be slick."

"I'll call as soon as I get home." I hugged her. "Thanks for everything."

"You're welcome," my mother said, biting down on her lip. "Thank *you*."

"I love you, Mommy," I said, fighting tears.

"I love you, too, Livi."

My mother stood under a large black umbrella and waved until I turned the corner. For two nights and two days I was comforted by her cocoon, feeling as though I was nearly ready to emerge a butterfly. We revealed secrets and placed imaginary balms on pain. Opened sealed boxes and left them slightly ajar.

I wasn't certain if my father knew that I was gone or even had a sense that I had been there. Each time I leave them, still, I struggle with the thought that it could be the last time I see them. My father, of course, has faded before my eyes for the last two years. Mommy is another story altogether. For me, she is immortal and still omniscient.

CHAPTER SIXTEEN

Carl

Before I saw my mother, I stopped at a book shop and bought a dictionary. It was bound in dark brown leather, engraved with gilded letters and had large bold print inside, so unlike the paperback from long ago. The saleswoman wrapped it in tissue and tied it with strands of woven straw, explaining that twine and string bring better luck than ribbon.

I drove to the beige sandstone building with new windows framed in black steel and a lot of benches and greenery around the sides and back. I walked up to the front desk where a woman with blue hair wore an almost matching blue smock.

"How can I help you?" she asked.

"I am here to see Mary Lou Parker," I said.

I didn't say that she was my mother.

"Your name?"

I hesitated too visibly. If I gave my real name, I feared it could have been too much for Mama's heart. I was afraid if I said Carl Larkin, there was a chance the woman would have known him. I felt as persecuted and paranoid as I had when I was on the road at seventeen.

"Dean," I said, my pulse racing.

"And do you have a last name, Dean?" the woman asked with what I thought was an emphasis on "Dean."

"Moriarty," I said, shaking my head at the strange association.

The woman called upstairs and, as I expected, my mother said she didn't know a Dean Moriarty.

"Are you a relative?" the woman asked, covering the mouthpiece of the phone.

"She might not remember me," I said. "Is she clear?"

"Clear?"

"Her mind."

"Oh, very. Nothing's wrong with her mind."

I thought for a moment. "Tell her I've brought a dictionary for her."

The woman related the message, hung up the phone, and summoned the security guard, still clearly suspicious of me. "Mr. Perry, would you kindly escort Mr. Moriarty to room five-one-five, Mary Lou Parker?"

We rode the elevator in silence. The steel doors opened and I thought of how I once pictured Heaven's gates when I was a child. The guard led me down the hall to a corner room where "Mary Lou" was scripted in the center of a ceramic heart-shaped frame on the door.

"Miss Parker? You have a visitor," the guard called out, knocking and speaking as he opened the door.

She sat in a wheelchair by the window. She wore a yellow blouse, beige slacks, and white canvas sneakers, a pink blanket covering her knees. There was the ubiquitous paperback on her lap. Her hair was white, her eyes still that nearly iridescent turquoise. She was beautiful.

"It's all right, Mr. Perry," my mother said in the sweet tone I knew so well, yet as she spoke her eyes never turned from me. "You can go now, Mr. Perry."

As the guard left, I walked over to her. I was overcome. I kneeled beside her chair and placed my hands on her arm. "Mama. I promised I'd come back."

Her face was stained with tears although her body didn't shake or sob. She placed her soft hands on my face, as if she was making sure I wasn't an apparition. She drew circles on my cheeks with her palms and studied my face. And then she said, "I've been waiting for you, Joe."

CHAPTER SEVENTEEN

Olivia

The light still burned on the porch when I drove up to the house. Although I had no expectations, there was a pit in my stomach when Carl's car was not in the driveway. The mailbox shutter was pushed slightly open by two days' worth of mail—mostly Christmas catalogs and flyers promoting discounts. Nothing of importance except for bills. More to the point, no further communication from Carl. No messages on the machine. Not even from Ginny, and that was one I hoped for. It was my fantasy: *Hi, Miss Hughes. It's Ginny. Dr. Larkin is here. It turned out to be a business trip and he's buried under paperwork but he'll call you later.*

Emmet behaved strangely, or perhaps I was projecting. He sniffed about the house searching for Carl. There is a bond between the two of them, even more than the one that Emmet and I share. It was Carl who found him eight years ago, huddled and cold, in the doorway of a shuttered shop near the campus. No other pups, just Emmet—hungry, wet, and cold with a big round brown nose and such sad soupy eyes that Carl named him after Emmet Kelly, the morose clown who made people smile. Carl brought him home tucked inside his blue wool coat. There is a tremendous kindness in Carl's heart.

I taught my two o'clock class: Performance I. It doesn't get more basic than that. The class performed monologues and I could barely keep my mind from wandering as they droned on. The students seemed subdued and it occurred to me Carl's absence had probably become an embellished rumor.

I had an hour between class and rehearsal for *Antigone* so I went to Carl's office. The door was open and Ginny was at her desk, immersed in filling out a form on the computer.

"Ginny?"

She visibly jumped. "Have you heard from him?"

I nodded. "He should be back at the end of the week," I said, stretching the truth.

"Oh, thank goodness. Is everything all right, then?"

"He had some things he had to take care of," I said, trying to be casual.

"Nothing serious?" she asked. "I'm sorry. I don't mean to pry."

"No, that's OK. Any messages for him? I'll be happy to let him know . . ."

"Nothing that can't wait."

"Well, all right." I had little else to say.

"Miss Hughes? Are you sure there's nothing I can do?"

I cocked my head to the side, not knowing exactly what she meant.

"For you. You look, well, tired."

"I am," I said.

I turned my eyes away from her and looked down at her desk. There was a handwritten envelope addressed to Carl. It looked more like a personal note than a business note. The return address was from an Eleanor Martin in Warrensville, North Carolina. I picked it up. "What's this?"

"My guess is it's a note from that boy's mother. The one who changed his lab a couple of weeks ago?"

"He's from North Carolina?"

"Something like that," she said.

"Why would she write a note to Carl?"

"Southern hospitality, I suppose. She's probably thanking him for letting her son leave school."

"Isn't that rather unusual?"

"Well, yes. But the boy took off the day because a family member was ill so I suppose the mother felt she should write something personal."

"What's the boy's name?"

"Robbie Martin."

I placed the letter back on Ginny's desk. "Take care," I said. "We'll be in touch, right?"

🌀

I sat through *Antigone,* and where I typically would have had plenty to say—corrections, criticisms, suggestions—I was lost in my own world. In some ways, Antigone, like me, was involved in a triangle. And like me, one of those in the triangle was dead. In Antigone's case, it was her brother, whom she tried to avenge, making certain he received a proper burial. Her loyalty ultimately condemned her to death. God, I hated irony at that moment. Are we always condemned when we are seized with love and loyalty?

"Professor Hughes?" the girl who played Antigone asked. "Should we run it through again?"

I hadn't even noticed that rehearsal ended.

"Enough for today," I said. "Good job."

The cast whispered as I left the auditorium. I knew they were talking about me, but I didn't care.

I went to the library and pulled an atlas from the shelf. I opened it to North Carolina and found Warrensville. It was a town on Thunder River. I knew it sounded familiar. Nina and

Frank had gone there with Jillian last summer. I looked up Matthew's Hill where Carl had grown up. It was just west of Warrensville, not by more than twenty miles. My heart was pounding. It was all too coincidental.

Belvedere is a relatively small campus so Robbie Martin wasn't hard to find. I could have gone to administration or to the bursar's office, asked what dorm he was in, and made it simpler but I didn't want that much involvement. Considering that Carl was undoubtedly a rumor and I was the wife left behind, I didn't want to draw attention to myself. I walked over to Rumson, the science building, and figured I'd start with the small library on the second floor. There were two boys and a girl sprawled on a sofa in one of the study alcoves.

"Do any of you know Robbie Martin?" I whispered.

They pointed to an alcove on the far side where a blond boy sat in front of a computer screen.

I walked toward him and, although I wanted to talk with him, I realized there was nothing I could say. I mean, what would I say? *I'm Professor Larkin's wife and do you happen to know where he's gone since you're from neighboring towns?* So, I stood and stared at Robbie Martin. For the briefest of moments, I was back at the liquor store, compelled to stand where Noah had been gunned down. The same sort of feeling came over me as I looked at Robbie. Instinct told me that somehow, inadvertently, Robbie's appearance in Carl's office had triggered something within Carl. I couldn't shake the feeling that Carl had gone back home. The boy turned in his seat and stretched his arms over his head and, catching sight of me behind him, stifled a yawn in midair.

"Excuse me, ma'am," he said, clearly startled by my presence.

I smiled at him and walked away.

There were still no messages when I got home and suddenly Carl's absence frightened me. Or maybe it wasn't so much his absence as it was that, no matter how hard I had tried to convince myself he wasn't part of the fabric of my life for the last twenty-two years, I couldn't.

It felt like the fabric was unraveling thread by thread.

CHAPTER EIGHTEEN

Olivia

Carl still hadn't called by noon on Wednesday. I don't teach on Wednesdays, and usually sleep in an hour later and then grade papers for Dramatic Expression. I couldn't sleep and I couldn't concentrate to grade efficiently. The notion that he was "OK" was no longer enough. Men who take off for whereabouts unknown to their families are not "OK." And neither was I. Moment by moment, the cavalier attitude I tried to adopt was disintegrating.

Thanksgiving was two weeks away. We used to alternate homes each year for the feast—Nina's, ours, my parents—but since my father became ill, we went to Chatham. Travel was disorienting for my father, not to mention that he could no longer drive. Nina and I planned to make the pilgrimage to Chatham on Wednesday morning with Frank and Jillian, Carl and our kids arriving on Thursday morning. And now? I pictured our families watching football, the girls complaining about sports and playing Scrabble while my mother and Nina and I cooked. But what if Carl was still gone?

I stared at the phone, willing it to ring. Anything, even a wrong number, just to have a momentary hope.

I needed to do something mindless. I thought of baking pies for Thanksgiving and freezing them. I pulled the flour and brown sugar from the shelf but had no apples or cinnamon and not enough eggs. I reasoned with myself: The house would have been just as quiet on any Wednesday morning. Carl would be working and I would be savoring the "alone time," but there was no pretending that the quiet wasn't extraordinary that morning.

There are few sounds of emergencies in Willow. Our population is eleven thousand. We're a fairly sleepy town, what people call a bedroom community, and if not for Belvedere, the town would have even less bedrooms. Occasionally, in winter, I hear fire engines race by, usually because Christmas lights have flamed or flues have clogged. Typically, sirens are a rare occurrence in our town. That morning, while the weather was still unseasonably warm, the distinctive bleep of an ambulance broke the silence. I ran to the window and watched it speed by, lights twirling. I covered my mouth to suppress a cry. Emmet stood beside me, his tail low. He, too, was unnerved by the siren.

Emmet followed me up the stairs to the bedroom where my side of the bed was nearly untouched and Carl's not touched at all. I smoothed the spread and the bed was made. I looked around the room. The wallpaper was peeling in spots and the curtains were yellowed and tired. I walked the corridor to Sophie's room and then Daniel's, the bathrooms, opened the linen closet where everything was in sore need of refolding. I went downstairs and inspected the living and dining rooms and kitchen. Corners of the walls were chipped. The kitchen walls were splattered with grease. If I could paint the kitchen and add some wainscoting, cheer up the bedrooms with new duvet covers and curtains, paste down the wallpaper, perhaps it would be curative somehow.

I grabbed my handbag, felt around inside for my checkbook and wallet, and took my car keys from the hook by the door. I had just started the engine when I remembered my cell phone on the kitchen counter. It was ringing as I fumbled with my keys. By the time I got inside, the ringing stopped. The display read "one missed call" with a number that had a 910 area code. I dialed the number but it just rang and rang on the other end. I called the operator and asked where the area code was located.

Warrensville, North Carolina, she said.

I called my mother. "He's in Warrensville, North Carolina," I said breathlessly.

"How do you know?"

I explained the powers of the cell phone to her and how I tried to call back the number but there was no answer. I told her about Robert Martin and the proximity of Matthew's Hill.

"I don't understand," I said.

"Well, maybe the boy got him thinking."

"About what?"

"Well, he's from the same area of the country."

"So, why wouldn't he tell me, 'Livi, I'm going down South for a while. I need to think.' I mean, that's acceptable. And why's he in Warrensville and not Matthew's Hill? It doesn't make any sense."

"Well, first of all, Nina and Frank were down there last year and Warrensville is a popular resort town. And maybe he doesn't want anyone to know he's back so it's easier to stay a stone's throw away. As I said, maybe that boy got him thinking."

"About what? He left when he was seventeen. Do you mean to tell me that after forty-one years he can't tell me that he's going back there? He can't talk to me about this?"

"How often have you asked him?"

"I haven't."

"And, furthermore, it took you twenty-five years to go through the attic."

"So?"

"So, the past defines us. Doesn't matter whether it's twenty, forty, or sixty years."

"Do you ever get tired of being right?"

My mother laughed. "Tell me what you want."

"I want him to come home," I said.

"Well, now, that's progress," she said.

It wasn't until later that it dawned on me: When the ambulance raced by that morning, I didn't think of Noah when the siren pierced the air.

CHAPTER NINETEEN

Carl

The last time I saw my mother was forty-one years ago. She had strawberry-blonde hair that fell in curls to her shoulders. And a welt on her jaw that was a hideous shade of purple, and blood dripping from her lip onto the bodice of a sky blue dress. The last time she saw me, I had my father's blood on my hands.

That night, my mother was sitting in the living room, reading a book, waiting up for me as she often did back in those days. We'd chat a few minutes and I'd go to my room, so tiny there was just space enough for a bed and a night stand. Around two in the morning, I'd usually hear my father's car door slam and the muttering of obscenities as he staggered to the bedroom where he slept with my mother. It didn't matter if it was a Tuesday or a Saturday night, he'd finish at the paper mill and head right to the bar with the blue ribbon blinking in the window.

But the night that I left, my father was home before me, stinking of whiskey, his Bowie knife poised in his fist. Usually, the knife was strapped inside the brown leather case attached to his belt. I heard him shouting—about me—as I came up the walk.

I heard Mama begging him. "Calm down, now, Luther," she said. "He's just a boy."

I was strong then, and bigger than my father. I wasn't as afraid of him as I'd been when I was small.

I stood in the doorway and stared him down. "What's going on here?" I asked. "You have a problem with me?"

"Go to your room, Joe," my mother said desperately. "Just go and close the door."

"You take one step to that room and . . ." He ran his finger along the blade of the knife.

"Luther, don't. Don't talk like that," my mother said. She turned to me. "Joe, go."

"Mama's boy," he hissed. He put his face in mine. His breath stank of smoke and liquor and puke. "So, I hear you been hangin' out in Seaside."

"What's it to you?" I asked, turning my face from his.

"You shame my name and you ask what's it to me? You think 'cause you got some fancy scholarship that you're better 'n me?"

"I am better than you. Most people are better than you." I lifted my chin defiantly. "And what I do is none of your business."

"Joe, please. Don't talk back now," Mama chided, looking from one of us to the other, her eyes unable to avoid the knife in my father's hand.

"This is all your fault," he said, looking at my mother. "You with your books and your church. Letting coloreds in to pray. Ain't no place for coloreds in a white church."

"All people can pray in a house of God," my mother said softly. "God sees in color not black and white."

He spat on the floor and then turned to me. "You see in color, don't you Joe? You got yourself a colored girl. You gonna tell me it's a lie?"

Laura's words came back to me. *Nothing but trouble, Joe,* she would say to me as I kissed her in the car parked out on River

Road. Of course, deep down inside I knew she was right, but I loved her in the way that only a seventeen-year-old boy loves a girl. She was my world, my sanctuary, my prize, and the color of her skin made no difference to me. But I knew she was right. *We'll leave here together*, I'd say to her.

"I'm not talking to you." I started to walk away, toward my mother, but he pulled me back by the shirt.

"So, you tell me, Joe. What's colored pussy like? I'd like to know. Lotsa guys wanna know. The guys down at the bar wanna know. We're thinkin' we might all take a ride over there tonight and find that nigger girl of yours and git ourselves a little, too." He tightened his grip on the knife.

My heart throbbed through my chest. "You stay away from her."

"Aw, now whatcha gonna do, Joe? You her white knight?"

"You're drunk. You disgust me," I said.

"Joe, stop," my mother cried. "Luther! Leave him be now. You don't know what you're saying."

He grabbed my mother's arm. "You don't say nothin'," he said. "You don't open your mouth." He drew back his arm and hit her clear across the face with the back of his hand, the knife miraculously not slashing her face. Her lip split open and as she put her hand to her mouth, he kicked her in the hip and sent her sailing, sliding on the side of her face, across the floor.

I grabbed the back of his belt and pulled him before he could go near my mother again. I flung him around so he faced me, the Bowie knife glistening in his hand. I grabbed his right arm that held the knife with my left hand and twisted his arm behind him. We were face to face. I'm not too clear on exactly what happened after that. My father raised up his arm and the next thing I knew the knife was at the side of my neck as we struggled. My father stepped forward and forced me to step back and then, just as I felt the knife graze my neck, and felt a trickle of warm blood, I hurled myself toward him with all my might and shoved him into the cinder block wall. His head went back and he fell to the ground. Blood gushed down behind him and puddled on the floor. Hideous bursts spilled from his mouth and ear.

My mother crawled over, dragging her legs behind her as though they were lame.

My father wasn't moving. His eyes were glazed over, staring into space.

"Oh, sweet Jesus, what did I do? Oh, God. Mama." I fell to my knees.

"He's just drunk, Joe," she said, her eyes wide, her lip blown up the size of a balloon, her jaw abraded and already turning purple.

"No, Mama." I put my fingers to his wrist and then to the pulse on his neck. I thought I was going to throw up. "He's dead," I said. The knees of my jeans and my palms were wet with his blood. "I killed him."

My mother was sheet white. "You got to leave here now, Joe," she said. "You got to get out of here."

"It was an accident," I said, tears rolling down my face. "I just wanted to stop him. I was afraid he was going to kill you."

"I know that, Joe," she said, stroking the back of my head as I sat beside my father. "I was here, Joe. I saw."

"It was self-defense, then, right?"

"I'm not the one who needs convincing."

"So, we'll tell them, right? They'll understand, then, right?"

She shook her head. "You won't be able to convince the law. Not now. Too many folks know about you and Laura. You know this town, Joe. Even if a courtroom found you not guilty, folks'll come after you." She covered her face with her hands. "They'll kill you, Joe," she whispered. "You crossed the line, don't you see? You got to leave."

I blinked the tears from my eyes. "We were so quiet. No one knew. Just you and Laura's mother. That was all."

"Clyde Jenkins saw you two out on River Road tonight. He told everyone at the bar."

"How'd he see us? We were pulled way off to the side. And how come he didn't come to us himself?"

"More than likely Clyde was there with another man's wife. Or Lord knows what he was doing."

She started to get up from the floor and began to sway. "I need some ice. And a drink of water."

I wrapped some ice cubes in a dish rag. She held it to her lip and ran her tongue over her teeth. "No broken teeth, right?"

"No. You ought to keep the ice on there." I held the glass of water to her lips. "Here." She was a mess. "I can't leave you like this."

"You listen to me, Joe. You get as far from here as you can. I'm going to tell the police that I did it."

"You'll go to jail."

"No," she said firmly. "I got the lip to prove what he did to me. It was self-defense. They'll believe me."

"Not with me gone. They'll know it was me."

"They can believe whatever they like. I want you out of here. You've got to listen to me, Joe. You give me your bloody clothes and get out of here."

"Come with me," I begged. "I've got some money."

"Joe." She unclasped the St. Christopher medal from around her neck and hooked it behind mine. "Go. Just go." Tears poured down her cheeks. "Please. Listen to me. I love you, Joe."

"I love you, Mama. I'm going to come back for you. I swear."

I drove my car to Raleigh, ditched it on the side of Route 1, and hitched a ride to Rocky Mount, where I spent the night in a church. In the morning, a nun found me sleeping in the pew and awakened me. When she went to get me a cup of coffee, I

left. I hitched from there to Knoxville, Tennessee, and out to
St. Louis, stopping on the way at bus depots and train stations
that were warm enough to spend the nights and no one bothered me since most of those places were unmanned at night and
people often hung around, waiting for buses and trains and just
staying warm. I ate candy bars and drank Coca-Cola to keep
myself going.

I landed in Kansas City simply because I couldn't go any
farther. I got a job working in a barbecue place, and the owner
took a liking to me and didn't ask any questions. I had the
feeling he'd been in trouble once himself or maybe was even
running from something as well. He let me sleep on the con-
vertible sofa in his apartment above the restaurant until I had
enough money to rent a room at the YMCA. One day, without asking a question, he introduced me to a friend of his
who could get you everything from phony driver's licenses to
Social Security cards and passports. Nothing was tracked in
those days and false identification was easy to get. No compu-
ters. No picture identification. The counterfeiter had hair down
over his shoulders, a full beard, and wore a tight T-shirt with a
big peace sign on the front. His "operation" was in his basement. For fifty dollars, I got a phony driver's license and birth
certificate. The choice of name was up to me. "You best choose
someone dead," he said with no expression on his face and
handed me an obituary section from an old San Diego newspaper.

"Carl Larkin," I said, handing the paper back to him.

He scanned the paper. "No Larkin on here."

"It's OK," I said. "He's dead."

🌀

The law never believed that Mama killed Luther. She took
my blood-stained clothes and burned them in the stove and
flushed the ashes down the toilet. She took the knife and the

leather case from my father's belt and threw them in the Thunder River. She waited until nearly dawn before calling the police, and to this day I can't believe that woman had the strength and the courage to sit there with my father's dead and bloody body for that long.

She told the police she hadn't seen me since the morning before. "Luther came home drunk," she explained. "He got pretty steamed because Joe hadn't done his chores and Luther started to take it out on me."

She said that my father had more whiskey and when she suggested that she might take the truck and go and look for me he got real mad and cracked her across the face. That was when she pushed him, she said and, even though she was a small woman, it was mighty forceful, maybe because her adrenaline was flowing. Why, I never would have thought I had such strength, she said. They asked her why she wasn't crying and she said that when a woman gets beaten as much as she did the tears just dry up. Why, once he pushed me across the floor just 'cause he didn't much care for his breakfast.

The sad thing is, except for the fact that I killed my father, my mother's story wasn't at all that far from the truth.

The police went about the house and searched my room.

Sam Gibson was the investigating officer. He wasn't but five years older than me. He knew my family. He knew my father was what they called a hard-drinking man and he knew me well enough to know that my father and I didn't see eye to eye. Mama said he knew me well enough to know I didn't kill my father, but Samuel had a job to do. Sam also knew that I wasn't unfamiliar to the law. He knew I was capable of using my fists to avenge someone.

Sam said he was sorry for my mother's pain and asked if she wanted to go to the hospital but she declined, saying that ice and iodine should do the trick. But then Sam said he was obligated to take her down to the station if she was well enough. She went, willingly, and some other police talked to her and one of them gave her a polygraph test. My mother failed.

Sam took her aside after the test. "Where's Joe, Mrs. Parker? If you know where he is and you won't say, then you're obstructing justice and aiding and abetting."

My mother remained stalwart. She never wavered from her story. "I don't know where my son is," she said.

"You failed the test, Mrs. Parker. According to the test, your son killed your husband."

"Well, I cannot believe that you would believe some machine when I'm telling you what happened. That machine is broken. Or maybe it's just not accurate since I am so distressed."

"Why aren't you mourning your husband, Mrs. Parker?"

"You asked me that before," she said, looking him square in the eye. "I am sorry he's dead and I didn't mean to kill him, but I am glad he's the one who's dead and not me."

"And your boy? You ain't concerned as to where he is? About telling him that you've killed his father?"

"I told you everything there is to tell you."

"Well, we'll be waiting for Joe. And we'll be looking for him. Hunting for him."

"Why?" she asked.

"Because your son is a suspect in the murder of Luther Parker. And now your son is also a fugitive."

In the beginning, I called Mama every few weeks. I wanted to send money from my wages at the barbecue but she made me promise not to let anything come through the mail because everything had a postmark and that's how people left trails. Besides, she'd gotten a job caring for an older lady, and not only was she paid, but got three meals a day, and good ones at that. I asked the woman's name and she wouldn't tell me.

"The less you know, the better off you are," she said.

She had contacted Laura and told her what happened and, although Laura was distraught, she promised me that Laura was coming along. You tell her that I love her, I said. You tell her not to worry. It wasn't but a couple of months later that Mama heard through some folks at church that Laura's mother sent her to live with her aunt in Chapel Hill since she feared for Laura's safety. Threats were made against her by blacks and whites—both calling her names and accusing her of both betrayal and being with a boy she had no business loving. One night a cherry bomb was thrown through her bedroom window. That was when her mother sent her away.

I called my mother several times over the years, even though each time I could hear the fear in her voice, as if someone would burst through the door and find us out. I called when I started community college in Kansas and when I won a scholarship to KSU. I called when I got into the graduate program at MIT and told her I was getting my degree in physics, and although most mothers would have been so proud, she asked me why on Earth I wanted to be a scientist since I was meant to be a musician. I spoke to her when I got to Belvedere and told her the town where I lived and was about to give her my phone number when she told me to stop calling. She said that times had changed and there were electronic ways of tracing calls and I might be putting both of us in danger. I said that she was watching too much TV and reading too many crime novels but she was adamant.

The last time I spoke to my mother was nineteen years ago, right after Daniel was born. I told her about Olivia and Sophie and that I had a son and hoped he wouldn't turn out like me. And she said there would be nothing better on Earth than if he turned out like me. I asked if she thought he would be like Luther and she said that no child of mine or grandchild of hers could ever be like Luther. That Luther was the devil himself.

"I bet I could come see you, Mama," I said. "No one's looking for me anymore. No one remembers anymore. I even have a new name."

"Don't tell me what it is," she said. "You're just Joe and I don't want to know anything else."

She said that Samuel Gibson was chief of police now and although he never believed that she killed Luther, there was a look in his eyes that told her he forgave me, but maybe it was just wishful thinking on her part. For sure, if he ever found out where I was or if I ever came back he'd have to uphold the law. She reassured me that her friends, Imogene, Clara, Ettie, and Caroline were looking out for her. She even had a gentleman friend named Paul Sullivan who was a widower and Imogene's cousin. She said they had dinner at the diner and he treated her like a lady.

"What's he do for a living?" I asked.

Her voice faltered. "He's in the, um, tire business."

"Over in Raleigh?" I asked.

"Right," she said.

And although I never said anything, I knew there was no Paul Sullivan—that he was merely an invention to make me feel like some man was watching out for her.

"I miss you," I said.

"I miss you, too, Joe. Read the Bible, Joe. Read the story of Solomon's wisdom. I'd rather have you safe than here."

When I tried our number about six months later, it was disconnected.

It felt like a dream as I kneeled by her side. There hasn't been a night in forty-one years when she hasn't been in my thoughts as I fall asleep and with me again when I awaken.

"I got something for you, Mama," I said, placing the dictionary tied in twine on her lap.

"How did you find me, Joe?"

"Fate. Robbie Martin goes to Belvedere. It's where I teach."

"Oh, for goodness sakes. Robbie? He told you I was here? He knows about you?" She looked frightened.

"He doesn't know. And he doesn't know I'm here. No one knows. He needed permission to leave school to come see you. He mentioned your name." The dictionary was still on her lap.

"Open it, Mama."

Her fingers deftly unknotted the string and I was reminded of the way she let down the hems on outgrown clothing and threaded popcorn for the Christmas tree. Her knuckles were no longer smooth and her once alabaster hands were flecked with dark spots and swollen with age, but the same smile that always warmed my heart crossed her face and lit up her eyes when she saw the dictionary.

"Oh, Joe," she said, covering her mouth with her hands. "Why, it's just beautiful. It's a work of art."

And I laughed because she was always subject to hyperbole.

She opened the dictionary, shut her eyes and circled the page with her index finger, the way she used to, landing her finger on a word.

"Refrain," she said softly. "I know this one already." She read out loud anyway. "A regularly recurring phrase or verse especially at the end of each stanza or division of a poem or song."

Or as a verb, I thought. To stop oneself from following an impulse.

"I love you, Joe," she said and smiled. "Now that's a sweet refrain."

"I love you, Mama," I said.

"You're sure it's safe for you here?"

"It's safe, Mama," I said and, whether she believed me or not, she didn't protest.

There are certain defining moments in our lives and I knew that was one. I knew that I was Joe Parker. I had always been Joe Parker. We never really change.

CHAPTER TWENTY

Olivia

Carl has no photographs or mementos. No pictures of himself as a boy; no photographs of his parents. Nothing. Not even a high school yearbook. As for his college yearbook, he couldn't afford to buy one. His diplomas from Kansas State and MIT hang on the walls in his office, framed in old black wood and sorely in need of dusting. There is a bulletin board tacked with reminders for meetings, some of which have already passed, and an old snapshot of the children and me that's about ten years old. A long time ago, he said his memories are within him—that was the only thing the fire couldn't burn.

After the ambulance sped by the house, I went into Carl's den. The siren had stirred something in me that made me search for something that might explain his absence and, perhaps, his presence, as well. I opened his desk drawers and rifled through them with the desperation and anticipation of a thief. The bottom drawer of his desk contained a pile of unpaid bills and a manilla envelope with receipts. The top drawer held pens, pencils, rubber bands, and paper clips. There were journals and old news magazines. Nothing: Precisely what I expected to find.

I waited an hour or so, straightening out kitchen cabinets and drawers, beginning a task and jumping to another, not completing one of them. I kept hoping he might call. Silverware and

dishes and stained old plastic containers were spread about
the kitchen when I finally gave up, realizing I couldn't concentrate, and drove to the big shopping mall in Springfield. I
bought paint brushes, turpentine and paint—a gallon of Victo-
rian Peach for the kitchen, sandpaper blocks in different gauges,
a quart of enamel called Decorator White for the scarred trim
around the cabinets, sponges, and three rolls of paper wainscoting that looked like a garland of grapes and pears. I was suffi-
ciently armed with distraction to get me through what were
becoming endless hours of waiting.

Once again, the answering machine was blank when I returned. I covered the kitchen table with newspaper, filled a
bucket with warm soapy water, and began to wash down the
walls, realizing afterward that I should have sanded the walls
first. I dried my hands and turned on the small television on
the kitchen counter, clicking through the stations, but nothing captured my attention. While the section of wall dried, I
moved onto another corner, sanding the rough spots, feeling
the smoothness form under my fingers as I ran my hand over
the surface, the fine dust coating my fingertips. The phone rang.
It was Carl.

"Please. Don't be angry with me," he said as I picked up.
There was a softness in his tone that I'd never heard before.

"Where are you?" My heart pounded and I wondered if he
would tell me the truth.

He hesitated at first. "Warrensville, North Carolina."

"Why?" I thought about telling him that I found Eleanor
Martin's note but decided against it.

He sighed. "Why?"

"You always do that. You answer my questions with
questions."

"I don't mean to. It's so complicated, Livi."

Livi. He rarely called me Livi. Not in years, anyway.

"Are you OK?" I asked, and then before he could answer, "You're not OK."

He laughed. "And you answer your own questions for me."

"Are you?"

"I am," he sighed. "I know this is awful for you. I'm sorry. I am truly sorry."

"Why can't you just tell me what you're doing?"

"I will. I promise. I just can't right now."

"But you're not in any trouble. And you're not . . . "

"Despondent? No." He hesitated. I heard his breath catch. "If we turn our backs on our past, we lose our history. If we live in the past, we lose our future."

He could have been speaking in tongues.

My voice choked with tears. "What's going on with you? When will you be home?"

"A few days. What did you tell the kids?"

"I haven't told them anything. I just keep saying that you're working on a grant." A thought occurred to me. "They won't call your office, will they?"

"Not usually," he said thoughtfully. "You know what? Tell Ginny if they do, to just make me unavailable somehow."

"Can't you tell me anything at all?"

"I'm going to try to get home by Saturday."

A thought occurred to me. "Did you drive there?"

"I did."

"Why?"

"Why not?"

I laughed in spite of myself. "There you go again."

"Because I needed to—now this is going to sound very contrived—be on the road, so to speak."

"Like years ago?"

"Like years ago."

"So, then it has to do with all that?"

"It does," he answered with an obvious patience. "Livi, I promise you. I'm going to give you all the answers when I come home."

"So, you'll be home Saturday when?" I asked, realizing I needed to abandon my questioning.

"Evening more than likely. But I'll let you know. You'll be there, won't you?"

I nodded.

"Livi?"

"Yes, I'll be here."

"What's the matter other than the obvious?" he asked tenderly.

"You don't sound like you," I said, my heart racing.

"One thing I can tell you is that it's me," he said. "It's really me."

CHAPTER TWENTY-ONE

Olivia

Nina called, and although I typically tell her most things, I didn't tell her how I felt about the tone in Carl's voice. I didn't say that his voice was etched with tenderness or that he wanted to make certain I would be there when he came home. Somehow I felt entrusted with his heart and although I had no idea what it held within the chambers, for those few moments on the phone, I felt it was mine.

That night I dreamed that Carl was on his deathbed. But he wasn't Carl or human in any way. He was a merman, half man, half fish, and I knew it was because of that affliction that he couldn't move or rise or breathe without water. Each time I came to see him, he would inhale and tell me he would be all right, and each time I left his side, someone called for me to say that he was about to die. I woke up drenched in perspiration, feeling for the first time in twenty-five years the same instinct I had when the sirens raced by my apartment in Greenwich Village and, without knowing why, wove my way through the crowd because I knew in my heart that Noah was gone.

In the dream, I wanted to save Carl.

I have had bouts of similar instinct like that over the years, pertaining to Sophie and Daniel, although with Sophie, they've been less about the physical and more emotional. Sophie is less of an issue than Daniel over the years since Daniel is so much more physical and belligerent and I still worry that he will be in the wrong place at the wrong time.

Once Daniel took a baseball clean in the mouth at Little League. It shattered two baby teeth and split his lip, and although he was only fifteen minutes late coming home from the playground, I knew the reason was something other than just not watching the clock. I got in my car and drove to the field where Daniel lay on the ground. An elderly man, a retired doctor, in fact, lived in a house at the edge of the park, and was holding an ice pack on Daniel's mouth. Carl came with me but couldn't bear to look.

"He'll be fine," the doctor said. "He's a lucky boy. Doesn't even need a stitch."

Carl went to sit in the car. "I can't see him like that," he said. "Things with the mouth just do me in."

Carl stayed in Daniel's room after he was hit with the baseball. Carl lying next to Daniel on the bed, the two not speaking, watching some sort of baseball movie on television, and after Daniel finally fell asleep, Carl curled up beside him and fell asleep as well. There was a look of grief on Carl's face not in keeping with Daniel's relatively minor injury and yet I never asked him why.

I have tempered my instincts with Carl. One time his car broke down on I-91 coming back from Boston and although he was a good four hours later than I expected him to be, I never allowed myself to think something may have happened to him, though I cursed him for not carrying a phone.

I awakened in the middle of the night after the dream and, forgetting for a moment that he was gone, reached for Carl in the darkness. I have rarely allowed myself to cry over the years and even more rarely cried in front of Carl. I wept when the doctors told me about the hole in Sophie's heart and when

Daniel's mouth was hit with the baseball and I wept when they went off to college and for every milestone that came along for them before that. That night, I was afraid to cry over Carl.

I recalled the day of Millie's wedding when Noah's wedding band got tangled in Carl's shirt and the look on Carl's face when I said I was widowed and he asked how I was. It was that question which made me trust him enough to go to the dimly-lit bar. It was the two of us, the wind blowing outside, drinking martinis and telling just enough of the past where neither forced the other to exhume the depth of our pain. The wound of a fatal bullet, fire that turned Carl's life to ash. Interment of the past was simpler.

It was the only time we dared to open a window, and in the last twenty-odd years we have reached each other through a screen, filtering out debris that otherwise might come in on the wind.

The middle of the night is a treacherous time to think. Children often awaken with what the books on child rearing call "night frights," reducing those episodes to normal developmental behavior. My heart broke for my children when they awakened screaming from their dreams. It was nearly impossible to convince them that there were no monsters under the bed, that shadows on the walls weren't goblins or robbers.

If Carl had been there, I wondered if I might have crawled under the nook of his arm when I had the bad dream. Perhaps, but then with the sunrise I would have retreated again, pretending to be fearless and independent, not needing anyone but me.

I wondered if I failed at loving him or succeeded at withholding my love for him. Of course, both those things are the same.

I vowed that when Carl came home, I would tell him how dreadful it feels when once someone promised that together we would harness the wind, and then how it feels when he is taken away in the night. I would explain how difficult it is, after that, to believe in promises—how the hurt and fear was resurrected the morning Carl said "See you," and then was gone.

CHAPTER TWENTY-TWO

Carl

There are thirty thousand people in Warrensville. When I left, there were about fifteen thousand. Folks moved away, and so many of the people became what they call "the seasonals." Even when Olivia and I went to Chatham, tiny as it is, Olivia never ran into anyone she knew from "before." So, considering that when I left my hair was light brown and there wasn't a crease on my face, I assured myself that, forty-one years later, it was most unlikely that anyone would recognize me.

I hadn't counted on Sam Gibson. At sixty-three, Sam apparently never forgot a face.

After I left Mama, I went to the all-night drugstore and bought a razor since I left mine at home, and in walked Sam. Although I didn't recognize him, there was something familiar in the way he walked and held himself. Something that haunted me about his craggy weather-beaten face. What bothered me most about him was the way he looked me up and down as I paid at the register. He nodded to me and I nodded back and just as I thought he might say something, I got my change and headed out the door.

I drove back to the hotel and went up to my room and, from the window, I saw him waiting, I suppose, for me to get upstairs. He went inside the lobby and less than five minutes later, he was outside again, walking up the street to a black and white patrol car parked on the corner. My first instinct was to run, and then I realized that I was Carl Larkin with every form of identification—passport, driver's license, credit cards, even a birth certificate that validated my identity—so who was Sam Gibson to argue? Even if he had known Carl Larkin, the teacher—don't men sometimes have the same name?

The problem was that I was—I am—Joe Parker, and I was scared out of my mind.

I slept with my clothes on, sleeping more off than on. When dawn finally came, I told myself, he would have come for me by now if he knew who I was.

As promised, I went back to the care facility the next afternoon. I was hoping to take Mama out to dinner someplace but they wouldn't hear of it. She was doing well, they said, two more weeks and she would be discharged back to the assisted-living facility. The nurses said a dinner out could just set her back. That it was just a bit too much excitement. If they only knew.

Mama wished she could introduce me all over the place as her son Joe, but we both knew, despite my assurances, that it was still too risky.

"Say I'm your cousin Maddie's son from Milwaukee," I said.

She laughed. "Why on Earth would I have a cousin Maddie in Milwaukee?" she asked.

It occurred to me how accustomed I'd become to lying and how rapidly I could fabricate a self-protective tale. "Because Maddie doesn't exist," I said. "Because she can't be tracked."

She said nothing but touched the nape of my neck the way she had when I was a boy and said my name softly in that way that always calmed me down. Amazing how a man of fifty-eight could be reduced to feeling like a child with just a touch of his mother's hand and the softness of her voice.

We ate dinner at the facility and by eight o'clock Mama was ready for sleep. I waited in the hall while the nurse changed her and helped her to bed. I kissed her forehead and wished her sweet dreams.

"I'll be back in the morning," I said. "It's not too much for you, is it?"

"It's not enough for me." She smiled. "Hand me that book over there, would you?"

"You should get some rest."

"I always read before I go to sleep." She patted a spot on the nightstand. "And put that dictionary here, just in case."

"Mama? You ever hear from Laura Harris?"

"I've been waiting for you to ask. She's a pediatrician over in Chapel Hill. Married a nice young man and has two girls. She writes from time to time. When I had the heart attack last year, she came to see me."

"Does she ever ask about me?"

"Oh, yes," she said, her voice fading with fatigue. "We exhausted talk about that night, though. After awhile, we just moved on. She's a fine person."

"Well, good night, Mama," I said and kissed her on both cheeks. I wanted to ask more about Laura but I knew she was too tired. "I'll be back tomorrow."

It was just after nine when I got back to Warrensville. There was a little bar a few doors down from the hotel and I didn't feel like going back to my room. I wanted to call Olivia again but it was too difficult to have a conversation where I couldn't say anything. It would all just have to wait until I got home. I sat up at the bar and ordered a Jack Daniel's, my drink of choice forty years ago until I switched to martinis, a concerted and deliberate effort to erase any nuance, any link, any possible characteristic that I might have had in the past.

"Still like that Tennessee whiskey, Joe?" a voice behind me asked.

I turned around slowly and there was the man from the drugstore the night before. Unmistakably, Sam Gibson.

"I'm afraid you've confused me with someone else," I said in a vain attempt.

I moved to the end of the bar but Sam followed me. "The desk clerk told me your new name. Not too many folks left who remember Carl Larkin, but I do," he said. "He taught me in the tenth grade and then he taught my sister Lilly. Lilly's moved out to Raleigh now or else I'm sure she'd want to stop in and say hello."

I was perspiring.

"So, how're you doing, Joe?"

Don't answer him, I thought. He can't prove anything.

"Relax, Joe. It's OK." He took a swig of his beer. "You see your mama?"

I nodded. The charade was over.

"How's she doin'?"

"All right."

"What brings you back here after all these years?"

"I figured it was time." I took a drink of the whiskey. I looked him in the eye. "Why don't you just get it over with?" I was seventeen again. There was that cocky tilt to my chin, the pumping of the joint at the side of my ear over what was once an angular jaw. My arms felt strong and my stomach taut.

"I've been chief now for ten years," he said. "Next year I retire."

My pulse was racing. "You haven't answered me."

"In six months, I'm gonna retire. You know, years ago I wanted to lose that Luther Parker case, if you know what I mean. It missed the cutoff for the microfilm so all these years it's just been a paper file in archives. It's in what we call a sus-pended case file now. No one's come forward with any more information."

"I'm not sure I understand."

"The case hasn't been actively pursued in a lifetime, Joe.

Your missing person's report will stay open. You know, your mama filed one that night. We did find your car in Rocky Mount but no trace of you." Sam leaned over and looked me in the eye. "Your paper file disappeared last night after I saw you at the Rite-Aid."

"Why would you do that for me?" I asked in disbelief.

"Too long ago, Joe. You're talking forty-one years. No one's even talkin' about O. J. anymore and I still can't believe he was cleared. Ain't no one's lookin' for his wife's killer so you tell me why I need to bother with a piece of shit like Luther Parker."

Hearing my father's name made me wince. "There are other cops on the force who remember."

"The oldest cop on the force besides me is forty which means he wasn't even a gleam in his daddy's eye in nineteen sixty-five. No one's left to remember. They're either dead or moved on."

I still didn't trust Sam and the look on my face showed.

"This isn't just for you. It's for your mama. He would have killed one of you eventually. There was never any doubt in my mind that it was self-defense. Of course, mine wasn't the only mind set back then. You wouldn't have stood a snowball's chance in hell of winnin' that case. Justice system here wouldn't have worked for you."

"Because of Laura."

He nodded. "This was one nasty place back then. You mama was right making you to leave that night."

"She told you?"

He laughed. "Never. That woman never cracked. But I knew she gave you her blessing. You never woulda left her otherwise. Your daddy wasn't fittin' to roll with pigs."

I almost laughed. "I haven't heard that expression in a long time."

"So, why'd you take Mr. Larkin's name?"

I told him about the man in Kansas City with the roster of

obituaries. "I figured if I was going to take a dead man's name it might as well be Carl Larkin."

"You still play the piano?"

I shook my head. "Not since I left."

"What do you do?"

"I'm a scientist. A physicist."

"Well, I'll be darned. Why on Earth. . . ."

I smiled. "I took a whole other direction. Besides, there's lots of physics in music." I was about to explain and stopped. "My daughter is a musician."

"Well, I'll say. So, you're married?"

I opened my wallet and took out a photograph. "My wife, Olivia. Sophie and Daniel." I smiled, dreaming. "Daniel's going to be a politician, I think. Or maybe a lawyer."

"Nice family," he said.

"You?"

"I married Becky Henderson—you remember her? We started datin' in the eighth grade. Matter of fact, I think Becky and I got married right before you left town. Got three sons: Sam Jr., Pete, and Andy. Five grandkids. Only one girl amongst them, though. Guess we make boys in our family."

"Sure, I remember Becky. You two were a couple when I left town." I shook my head. "Jesus, Sam. We were both kids when I left and now you're a grandfather."

"You watch out or I might change my mind 'bout you." He winked at me. "How long you staying?"

"Another day or two." I signaled the bartender. "Two more rounds."

We got our drinks and Sam raised his glass to mine. "You know, I always thought his name should have been Lucifer Parker."

"Look, I don't know what to say. . . ."

"I didn't do nothin' that shouldn't be done from the git go."

"What do you think might have happened if I'd come back

to see Mama years ago?" I asked. "I wanted to. She wouldn't let me come back."

"Clive Jenkins was still around then. About five years ago, he got drunk and wrapped his truck around a tree and that was the end of him." He popped a handful of pretzels into his mouth. "Clive wouldn't let it go. There's no statute of limitations on killin'. Even when it's self-defense."

"So, I did the right thing, then?" Finally, I accepted that he believed me.

Sam placed his hand on my shoulder. "Joe, you did the only thing you could do. You did what I woulda done, too." He called the bartender one more time. "We're celebratin'. This here's an old friend."

He raised his bottle to my glass. "You're home free, Joe. God bless."

I shut my eyes, "Thank you, Sam."

I went back to my hotel room, reeling from the whiskey and picturing myself as a jigsaw spread out on the cement floor of my childhood home. Bits and pieces of who I was and continued to be were put in place. I could feel myself slowly becoming whole. The temperature had dropped and an icy rain pelted the pavement. I remember thinking that Hell finally froze over.

CHAPTER TWENTY-THREE

Olivia

I taught my class on Thursday and sat through yet another rehearsal of *Antigone*. I stopped at the market and picked up milk, bread, eggs, fresh mozzarella, and two tomatoes and went to the liquor store where I bought a bottle of Pinot Noir. The sequence brought me back to the Jefferson Market. I pictured myself twenty-five years before, carrying my small bag of groceries, heading home, and bounding up the stairs to prepare dinner for Noah and me. It was the first time I was able to look back on those days with fondness, a sweetness in my heart, a peace in my soul that didn't make me cringe. Maybe, I thought, maybe I had finally found a corner of my heart for Noah.

As I unpacked the few groceries, I thought of Carl wending his way home from Warrensville, pictured the traffic on the highway and, still not knowing what he was seeking or what he discovered in Warrensville, wondered whether he would make the trip easily and uneventfully. In other words, I allowed myself to worry, to wonder, to wring my hands. To be his wife.

I finished painting the kitchen that night. I worked late, until nearly two in the morning. I pasted the wainscoting along the walls, shined the cabinets with an old can of Preen that I found under the kitchen sink, and lined the drawers with contact paper. I was just about to get into bed when the phone rang. My heart stopped. A phone ringing in the middle of the night is never good news.

"Hey," the voice said.

It was a man's voice. I nearly hung up because I thought it was a wrong number. "Who is this?"

"Me."

"Carl?"

"Yup."

I sat up in bed. "You sound funny."

"Maybe I am funny."

"Oh, for God's sake. You're drunk!" I said, crawling under the covers. "You've been drinking martinis."

"Whiskey," he said and then he laughed. "Jack Daniel's."

"Who's that? Your new best friend?"

"So, what have you been up to?"

It was crazy. He was acting like everything was routine. "Painting the kitchen. Fixing up the house."

"Industrious."

I didn't want to be sarcastic but I couldn't resist. "You see, I'm married but my husband decided to take off for parts unknown last Friday so I'm trying to keep busy, you know?"

There was silence.

"Carl? Are you there?"

"I guess." He yawned. "Hey, you know what they call that iced tea your mother makes?"

"What?"

"Down here. Do you know what they call it?"

"Iced tea?"

"Sweet tea," he said, mocking a southern accent. "Down here they call it sweet tea and you wash down a hoecake with it."

"What's a hoecake?"

"A scone. You New Englanders call it a scone."

I laughed. "You sound like one drunk Southern boy."

"I am a Southern boy," he said seriously.

"You're a *drunk* Southern boy," I said. "Did you run into an old drinking buddy?"

"Sorta," he said, slurring the word.

I swear I heard him snore for a second. "Carl?"

"Huh?"

"You OK?"

"You already asked me that."

"Well, I'm asking again."

"I'm falling asleep, Livi. I'll call you."

"When?"

"Tomorrow."

I couldn't fall back to sleep after Carl's call. I went downstairs, Emmet at my heels, and put on the kettle for tea. Yellow lights flashed through the kitchen window and then there was a rumbling of metal on metal, a crashing sound. I parted the curtains and looked outside. There was a thick cover of snow and more coming down. The sound and the lights belonged to a plow. It must have been snowing for hours. Emmet began to whimper so I let him out the back door, holding it open while he scurried to a favorite spot, watching as he shook the snow off his back and lumbered back inside. I poured my tea and sat at the table, admiring my handiwork. There was something about the smell of fresh paint that made me feel hopeful. Emmet rested his chin on my lap, a posture usually reserved only for Carl.

I stroked Emmet's head. "I miss him, too," I said aloud.

CHAPTER TWENTY-FOUR

Olivia

What started as a typical New England snowstorm became a blizzard by Friday morning. I slept through my alarm. Instead of hitting the snooze button at six-thirty, I must have shut it off. The next thing I knew it was nine-thirty. My class was at ten but the recorded announcement when I called the college said that campus was closed and, gratefully, I fell back on my pillow. Emmet, however, nudged me, so I put on my coat over my pajamas and took him outside. Emmet should live in Miami or something. He took one look at the snow, did what he had to do, and came back inside.

I called my parents and predicted that my mother would say she had a beef barley soup simmering on the stove and the two were nestled in snug as bugs. She said the Sound looked like a picture postcard (is there any other kind?) and that Nina had already called. Jillian's school, of course, was cancelled and she and Frank were out sledding. Nina was baking oatmeal cookies.

"Have you heard from Carl? The Weather Channel says the storm is coming up from the Carolinas. "

"He called last night. He didn't say anything about a storm." I didn't tell either Nina or my mother that he was drunk, just that he'd be home on Saturday.

"That's tomorrow," my mother said.

Strange, I'd lost track of the days.

I contemplated taking my Jeep and going somewhere. Anywhere, just to get out of the house. I found myself envying Carl's mystery trip, saturated with whiskey, in a small romantic southern town.

I thought of braving the road to Home Depot and buying paint for the vestibule (I'd seen one that was a bold rose color and hadn't had the nerve to buy it the last time I was there) or maybe get new bedspreads and curtains at the bed and bath shop, but I was too weary. Besides, it wasn't exactly the adventure I had in mind. I brewed a pot of coffee and turned on The Weather Channel, thinking that eventually we all become our mothers, picturing my mother stirring the soup, no doubt watching The Weather Channel on that antiquated television in her kitchen.

My mother was right: The meteorologists, what they call weather people when a storm hits, were tracking this Nor'easter from the Carolinas to New Hampshire. There was so much ice in Raleigh that power lines were down and phones knocked out. One of the "storm chasers" was standing along a highway, cars spun out around him. He looked like a hologram standing in the snow that blew in different directions all around him. "One of the worst storms we've had in years," he said. The feed failed and the man was gone. I told myself that The Weather Channel always makes everything sound worse than it is when it's bad enough.

I wished I knew exactly how long a drive it was from Warrensville to Willow.

The original number was still on the caller history of my cell phone, although the others have come up with an unavailable ID. Just for the hell of it, I dialed and the phone rang a dozen times before a woman answered. She had a pronounced southern accent and sounded older. I asked if I had reached a hotel or someone's residence and she said it was a cardiac care facility.

"Where?"

"Leland."

"Where's Leland?"

"North Carolina."

"Near where?"

"Well, about two hours from Raleigh. Half hour from Warrensville. You've dialed a pay phone, Miss," she said.

I asked for Carl Larkin but she knew no one by that name.

"But he called me from there," I said.

"Well, we gets lots of visitors," she said sympathetically.

"Is the weather really bad?" I asked.

"Oh, it's pretty icy and there're some outages here and there," she said. "But there's no one on the roads. Where're you?"

"Massachusetts."

"Well, my word! You got someone here, honey? 'Cause if you do, everyone's all tucked in and we got a generator so there's nothing to fret about."

I wondered what kind of husband doesn't tell his wife where he is staying and what kind of wife doesn't insist upon knowing. I felt my heart sink.

I thanked the woman and hung up, wondering why, of all places, he had called from a cardiac care facility. It crossed my mind that he went back home to have some sort of invasive surgery and then I reminded myself that cardiac patients don't call up drunk at two in the morning.

The phone rang and it was Daniel. "Some weather, huh?" he said as I answered.

"Pretty, though." I tried to sound cheerful. "The river is frozen solid. There were even some skaters out this morning."

"I take it the campus closed. Ours did."

"Thank goodness, because I slept through my alarm. Well, we'll have a nice long weekend this way," I said.

"Where's Dad?"

"Sleeping. He has a touch of the flu. It started last night."

"I haven't spoken to him all week."

"He's been writing grants. You know how he gets."

There was silence and then, "What aren't you telling me, Mom?"

"Telling you what?" Here it comes, I thought.

"It's not grants."

"He went to Warrensville last Friday, Daniel," I confess.

"So why didn't you say so? What the hell's in, what, Warrensville?"

"Yes."

"Yeah, so what's there?"

"That's where he went."

"Mom, this is like 'who's on first.' "

I laughed.

"It's not funny. Why the big secret?"

"It's not."

"Apparently it is. Is he OK?"

"He's fine."

"So . . . oh, for Christ sake, forget it."

"Daniel, I don't why he's there. He's going to tell me when he gets home. Tomorrow. He left last Friday and that's all the truth I know." Yes, I thought, except for the fact that I didn't know he was leaving.

"And I'm not supposed to think that this is fucked up?"

"I hate when you speak that way."

"He pisses me off."

"Why?" I asked gently.

"Because he's not honest. He doesn't speak his mind."

"That's not so, Daniel. Maybe it's just not always what you want to hear." It is my mother's voice in mine. "Give him a chance to explain before you condemn him." He doesn't answer me. "Don't be angry."

I've always worried about Daniel when he is angry. I worry that he will get in his car and take off down the road, his foot to the accelerator, not paying attention. My mind wandered and I began to feel panicky. "Daniel, please, everything's going to be fine."

He was sullen. "Look, just call me when he gets back."

"I promise," I said. "Try to take it easy."

"I don't get him, that's all." He paused. "And he doesn't get me."

I didn't have the strength to argue. "He *does* get you. He loves you. And I love you, Daniel. Take care of yourself."

"Yeah, right."

"Daniel! Don't do this."

"Love you, too, Mom, OK? " he said and hung up the phone.

I called Sophie. She was on her way to the corner coffee house with friends and then to the video store. They had a snow day planned—videos and carbohydrate loading, she said with a giggle. She is happy and distracted. No questions asked.

I felt claustrophobic and yet leaving the house was out of the question. Had I left the hour before, I would have found myself stranded in Springfield. I took down the curtains from every window in the house. They are sheers and wash easily, no ironing. I tossed them in the machine and watched the hot water run over them as years of grime loosened from the fabric. Pathetic, I thought, that this was somehow satisfying.

I decided to surprise Carl and clean his den—at least that's what I told myself, and believed my own lie. Armed with rags and furniture polish, glass cleaner, and my trusty new bucket filled with pine cleaner and water, I wiped the top of his desk and put papers in piles, paper clipped little scraps in neat bundles, opened the drawers I had just opened a night or two before, and arranged pen and pencils and rubber bands.

The deep walk-in closet reeked of mothballs and was lined with discarded clothing that Carl saves because he contends it will come back in style. The closet shelves were laden with file boxes and old journals. I pulled things down and placed them back, wiping the shelves clean in the process and then, down on my knees, pulled out more boxes from the floor of the closet marked "duplicate copies of grants" stretching back to Carl's MIT days. There was a wooden tennis racket with broken strings, shoe boxes of baseball cards that belonged to Daniel and, way in the back, a freestanding steel safe where we keep documents—wills, tax returns, birth certificates. I wrung out the rag and passed it behind the safe to collect the dust. My hand touched a pair of shoes and I pulled them out. Old, black canvas Converse sneakers, the soles covered with grime. I didn't know that Carl owned old sneakers like those. I clapped one against the floor to loosen the dust and a yellowed slip of paper fell out. A receipt from a Sinclair Oil station but I couldn't make out the amount or find a date since the carbon was smudged. I slapped the other sneaker against the floor and a gold medallion on a greasy tangled gold chain fell out: a St. Christopher medal, inscribed on the back with the name Mary Lou.

I placed the paper and the medallion back inside the sneakers and shoved them behind the safe, my hands shaking, gathered my cleaning supplies and put them away.

That was my punishment, I thought. Under the guise of cleaning, I was searching. Snooping. And now I wondered if Mary Lou was the reason that Carl went back to Warrensville or Matthew's Hill or wherever he was. If she was the girl he left behind. If Mary Lou was the only living memory he had after the fire.

CHAPTER TWENTY-FIVE

Carl

By Friday morning the hotel had lost power and phone service. I remembered from my childhood how the pocket between the river and the beaches always got socked really hard when any kind of weather rolls in, so it was no surprise.

By late afternoon, I braved my way to Leland. What normally would have been a fifteen-minute drive took over an hour, what with folks spinning out and emergency vehicles blocking the roads, not to mention that the ice was slick to negotiate, even for a seasoned New Englander like me in a four-wheel drive. Typically, the storm was heading north and by my estimations should have rolled in to Willow just about then. I thought of Olivia and hoped one of the neighbor kids would help her dig out if it got really bad. I smiled to myself, though, because knowing my wife, she'd probably set to do it herself, standing out there in a tank top like she did last winter saying the best thing about a woman's middle age were the warm surges that got her through the worst of the cold. Her personal furnace, she called it. I don't think my southern blood ever stopped running through my veins because the cold has always gotten to me, freezing every muscle in my body.

Mama was in her room, waiting for me. She wore a soft sky-blue turtleneck sweater and a beige skirt that fell to her ankles.

Her hair was swept up in what I think is called a chignon, and she had on a trace of pink lipstick.

"Well, if that sweater doesn't light up your blue eyes," I said. "You're still a beauty, you know." I kissed her cheek.

"I heard the roads are bad," she said. "You took a chance coming here."

"Neither rain nor sleet nor snow," I said. "How are you today?"

"Every day's a little better. I should be back at The Nightingale on Wednesday. At least that's what the doctor said this morning." She sniffed. "Personally, I think I should have been out of here last Wednesday but the Martins think this is best."

I tried not to look crestfallen. The Martins were living my life.

"Well, that's a pretty name, The Nightingale."

"After Florence. It's not a nursing home, you know. It's assisted living," she said emphatically.

"You like it there, Mama?"

"Oh, I like it fine. It's busy and the staff is real nice. Imogene's there, you know. She's got Parkinson's now but her mind's still clear. Clara's husband passed so she's out in Okracoke with her sister. Ettie passed several years ago and Caroline and Wayne are down in Jacksonville." She took a deep breath. "We all keep in touch, though."

"I have a picture," I said, reaching for my wallet. "The kids are big now. Sophie is twenty and Daniel is nineteen."

"You're still with your wife, I hope."

"I am."

"Well, that's good. Everyone's getting divorced these days."

I handed her the photograph and she studied it for a long time. "Tell me about them."

"Sophie is a musician and Daniel . . . " I laugh. "The jury's still out on Daniel but he's got a fire in his soul and a big mouth to go along with it."

"Remind you of anyone?" She smiled.

"I've changed."

"No one ever really changes. You've tempered, perhaps. Now there's a word I learned just last night."

"Well, I've tempered, then." I cleared my throat. "Mama, I ran into Sam Gibson last night. He got rid of the file."

Mama paled. "What file?"

"It's OK," I said quickly. "Everything's fine. The file from that night. He let it go. Lost it, he said."

"They keep those things on microfilm," she said knowingly.

I smiled. "You amaze me," I said. "How do you know about microfilm?"

"They use it at the library," she said shyly. "I still have my library card, Joe."

"Well, the file missed the cut-off for microfilm. It was just a paper archive. Sam swore to me. There's nothing there now."

"And you believe him?"

"Absolutely."

"He shouldn't have waited so long," she said angrily.

I didn't want to upset her. "He did what he had to do all these years, Mama. Sam's a good guy."

She sighed.

"It doesn't matter now, Mama. It's over." I said. "I suppose Sam thought I wasn't coming back or he would have gotten rid of the file sooner. But it's gone now."

She looked back at the photograph in her hand. "Tell me about Olivia."

"We met at a wedding in Boston."

"Meeting at a wedding's always a good sign." She smiled. "She catch the bouquet?"

"No, but I guess it didn't matter too much." I was lost in thought.

"What's the matter, Joe? I can read you like a book."

"What kind of book? Mystery?"

"Don't be smart. No, for me you're easy reading. So, are you going to tell me?"

"I never told Olivia about me. She doesn't know my real name. She doesn't know about Luther."

"Well, where does she think your family is?"

"I said that you and Luther died in a fire." I looked down at my hands. "I never even told her your real names."

My mother's face was stricken. "Why wouldn't you tell your wife? Now, husband and wife are supposed to be family. There's supposed to be a trust there. That's no recipe for a marriage."

"I didn't want her to know I killed my father."

"It was self-defense, Joe. I was there. If you hadn't done it, he would have killed *me*."

"There were times I thought I could tell her. Times I started to and then just stopped. I thought I might lose her. She married Carl Larkin. When I fell in love with her, I was Carl Larkin."

"Carl Larkin is only a name."

"I know."

"Are you planning to tell her the truth when you get home?"

"That's the plan," I said, walking to the window and looking out over the snow-covered lawn.

"Does she know you're here?"

I nodded. "But she doesn't know why. I didn't lie, though. I said I had things to tend to."

Mama shook her head. "Partial truth. Not the same as the whole truth so help you God."

"They don't use the Bible in courtrooms anymore."

"Well, maybe they should."

"I wanted to be someone else with her. Someone entirely different."

"Well, that's impossible," she said. "I would think you'd have known better."

"You think it's too late now?"

"Why, I never said that. Joe, you still wear that St. Christopher medal I gave you?"

"I have it," I said. "I put it away when I became Carl Larkin."

"You *never* became Carl Larkin," Mama said, her chin tipped up defiantly. "Not for one second."

There was a cacophony of voices out in the hall. Laughter and greetings. Someone saying they got in on Thursday just before the storm and practically skated here this afternoon. Footsteps came down the corridor and stopped outside the door to Mama's room with a rapid knock on the door.

"Mary Lou?" A woman came in, talking a mile a minute, taking off her hat and shaking off the snow.

"Laura?" I asked. She was older yet to me she was barely more than sixteen.

She looked at me and her eyes grew wide. "Joe?" she asked not above a whisper.

I took her hand. "It's been a long time."

"Yes, it has," she said, not taking her eyes from mine.

CHAPTER TWENTY-SIX

Olivia

The snow subsided by Friday night, although the forecast called for another storm on the heels of the one already blowing through. Strange how the fall had been so mild when it heralded a winter filled with such vengeance.

I called Nina around eight o'clock on Friday night and wished that she lived closer, down the street or in the next town, and not two hours away. We spoke for a few minutes but she and Frank had neighbors over. They were all sitting around the fire, drinking Irish coffee while their kids played in the basement. Nina is far more social than I. She's always giving dinner parties and getting involved with charity events and fundraisers. It's not that she's a socialite, just social. She runs a daycare center and I've often thought that's because, after Jillian was born, she and Frank tried for years to have another baby but it never happened. Nina doesn't talk about it. There is the stoicism, steeped and brewed within us.

Except for Nina and my mother, I have no confidantes, something that has become a liability as I've gotten older. I have acquaintances, friends I've made through the children, through their school, and colleagues at Belvedere, but no one with whom I am intimate. A half dozen or so good girlfriends drifted away after Noah was killed. They are really not to blame—I was less approachable and certainly less trusting of friendships when I became The Widow. Millie and I stay in touch, although she and Tom moved to San Francisco about eight years ago and distance makes the friendship difficult.

Carl told me about several girlfriends in college and graduate school and, until he met me, he was certain he would be an avowed bachelor. Once, he came close to marrying but the hours spent on his doctorate and then the sudden move to Belvedere interfered with the relationship. These were things he told me early on in our relationship—in the days when we confided bits and pieces, the perfunctory attempt to know each other better. He never told me the name of the girl who came close, though. And I never asked.

I lit a log in the fireplace, haphazardly surrounded by kindling and crumpled newspaper, and hoped it would catch. Carl was the expert at making fires, something I often thought was rather eerie given his history. Perhaps making fires was his way of taking control over what once took away his life. The fire strained to ignite as I poured a generous glass of red wine and sat on the floor, waiting. Suddenly, the flames burst and soared toward the flue.

I stared at the fire, lost in thought. Part of me coveted Carl's ability to take off the way he did and chase down whatever it was that he was pursuing, or perhaps confront what was pursuing him. Until recently, I didn't understand the reason why I was compelled to go back to the liquor store after Noah was killed. I have come to believe that it was for the same reason that people tie yellow ribbons around trees and place flowers and photographs at accident sites and build memorials. Those shrines are to make sure we never forget, to let the dead know that we remember just in case there is the slightest chance that they can hear us, see us, feel us. I wondered if Carl's house in Matthew's Hill was replaced by another, and if he stood on the site anyway or just walked streets he'd walked years ago and looked up names in the phone book to see who might be left.

Maybe he went to the cemetery to see his parents' graves or the church, although Carl has never set foot in a church for as long as I've known him except for the day we were married. My parents and Nina and Frank stood in a circle around us and we all held hands until Carl and I took our place in front of the minister. Afterward, we all went to dinner, and although it was just the six of us, it was meaningful. We didn't need gifts and well-wishers. It was just what we both wanted. And then Carl and I spent a long weekend at an inn in Provincetown where, yes, we made love in the darkness and roamed the beach at dawn and walked through the galleries and shops during the day. Our conversations were spare that weekend but in the silence there were words unspoken that we probably should have listened to more carefully.

We have one of those black plastic eight balls on the shelf in the living room. The kind where the answers float into a plastic window. ASK AGAIN LATER. YES, DEFINITELY. OUTLOOK NOT SO GOOD. Nina bought it for Carl one Christmas when he was particularly tormented over an NIH grant, waiting for it to come in. At her urging, he asked about the grant and the ball said REPLY HAZY. TRY AGAIN. Carl put the ball on the shelf, saying he could have made that prediction himself. I was trying to get pregnant at the time and I asked if I'd ever have children, not aloud, but whispered in another room. YES, DEFINITELY. But it didn't tell me about the hole in Sophie's heart or how it feels to have a life growing inside of you, a heart beating with your own that still beats to your rhythm even when the child is far away.

Of course, all questions for the eight ball have to be yes or no questions. The eight ball's prescience doesn't allow for explanations, reasons, or subtleties. The fundamental drawback, of course, is that the human spirit cannot be unequivocally reckoned and subject to simple, one-dimensional answers. It is far too embroidered, too rich in texture. As for predictions, they're not guarantees.

Had I asked the eight ball years ago if my father would be mentally intact in his old age, the ball might have said DON'T COUNT ON IT or OUTLOOK NOT SO GOOD. But it wouldn't have told me to notice that my father's hands always smelled like roses in summer or reminded me to watch carefully as he painstakingly laid slate for the path to our house in Chatham. It wouldn't have warned me to savor every embellished war story and cliché or predicted how deeply my mother would still love him even after his mind was gone.

Of course, the eight ball is nothing more than a toy and there is more to life than yes-and-no answers.

The cycle of the seasons is the one reliable prophet we have. It is the one pure indicator of the incarnations we can experience within our lifetimes. Fall was once a time when we cut back the roses and planted bulbs. Winter when we covered the shrubs with green canvas and placed a tarpaulin over the Roadmaster. Spring gave promise when the tulips and narcissuses bloomed along the slate path. Summer when the Sound was warm and we swam in the coves and fished off the pier. And then we started all over again feeling the dependability of sameness.

Despite my better judgement, I took the eight ball from the shelf and asked if everything would be right with Carl and me once he came home and it said CANNOT PREDICT NOW, probably the most honest answer I could have received from the eight ball. I took it as gospel though, directing me to capitulate to uncertainty and live in the present, allowing the past to nourish me with wisdom while I tried to hold out guarded hope for what was to come.

CHAPTER TWENTY-SEVEN

Olivia

A blanket of snow tumbled down to the river bank like rolled gossamer, untouched, perfect, and glistening in the sun. The river was still and laden with ice and the trees hung heavy with what appeared stalactites, frozen rapiers. Within hours, the snow would begin again. Willow is as beautiful in winter as it is in spring. It occurred to me as I gazed across the vista that Willow had become nearly as comforting to me as the Cape.

I realized that I needed to go back to Chatham and bring home the trunk and boxes from the attic. They belonged with me, along with the windmill. I wanted my wedding band and Noah's, the letters, the books and records, the snow globes and spoons. I wanted all of my life back and I wanted to bring it *home.*

I called Sophie before her eleven o'clock call.

"Did I wake you?"

"Sort of," she said sleepily. "What's going on, Mom?"

I decided not to tell her I was going to Chatham. "I just wanted to make sure you're not snowed in."

"Yeah, Boston does fine in the snow. How about you?"

"Good. Dad's out shoveling."

"OK, so, listen, I'll call you later. I'm going back to sleep."

I didn't bother to call my parents. My mother would have worried that the roads were icy. Never having been a driver, she became particularly panicked when there was any sort of inclement weather. As it turned out, the main roads were dry and well-traveled. There was no traffic. It took me three hours and I was there before two.

I smelled the barley soup as I came up the slate path. My mother was sitting in the kitchen, still in her robe, looking for the first time like a woman her age.

"For goodness' sake," she said, jumping up as I walked in the door. "How did you get here?"

"Car," I said. "What's wrong?"

"But the roads . . ."

"Don't believe everything you hear on TV. Too much drama. You look . . ."

"Awful?" she asked wryly. "We had a bad night."

"Why? Where's Daddy?"

"Sleeping, thank goodness. He has dreams. Nightmares." She sighed. "He has a hard time separating reality from dreams. My God, he's still so strong physically. He was flailing around and carrying on. It was all I could do to contain him."

"You should have called."

"It was four in the morning. What were you going to do?"

"You could have called the neighbors."

"Livi, please. There's something to dignity, you know."

"Maybe he needs to be in a . . ."

"It's out of the question," she said, preempting me. Her tone was sharp. "In a *home*? Euphemism for abandonment. That would kill him."

"This is killing *you*," I said softly.

She smoothed her hair with her hand. "I'll be fine. I need to bathe, that's all. And put on some decent clothes."

"I suppose I should have called first."

She waved her hand. "It's all right. I thought Carl was coming back today."

"Tonight. Not until tonight. And I'm sure the weather will detain him a bit. The storm is up and down the coast."

"What *are* you doing here, Livi?" she asked.

"Visiting," I said brightly.

She tsked. "To think, once you thought you'd have a career on stage."

"I want my things."

"Your *attic* things?"

I nodded. "All I took was the windmill."

"What brought this on?"

I told her about the medallion.

"So what?" she asked.

"So, he never told me anything about anyone named Mary Lou."

"You are the pot calling the kettle black," she said, shaking her head. "You haven't changed one bit, do you know that? You are the same obstinate, feisty little girl you were when you told us you were going to school in New York City and you were going to have your name in lights."

I smiled. "I thought I never gave you an ounce of trouble."

"Really? You moved in with Noah three months after you met him and if you think for one moment that your father and I didn't know, you're wrong. And you went to that college to begin with against our wishes."

"Well, you and Daddy agreed to pay for it."

"Because it was either that college or you wouldn't go to college at all. That you'd just waitress and become an actress anyway." She sniffed. "It was practically blackmail."

"What else?" I asked, as though I was listening to a story about someone else.

"What else? Oh, I don't know. Everything." She laughed. "Nothing. You were a handful. All emotion. Passion. And then when Noah died . . ." She stopped.

"Go on, " I urged.

"All the fight went out of you."

"So who am I now?" I demanded.

"Your own worst enemy," she said pointedly. "You're on your own in the attic this time. I don't have the strength."

I started toward the stairs. "Mommy? Have I really changed that much?"

"Oh, you're somewhere in there," she said.

My mother will never cease to amaze me.

My father awakened as I loaded the last box into the car. He stood in the kitchen, at least two days' growth of stubble on his chin, his hair mussed. He wore a tattered plaid robe tied too high on his torso.

"What are you doing here?" he asked.

"Taking my boxes from the attic."

"What for?" he growled.

"I just want to have them."

"What's in 'em?"

"Things from my apartment in the city." What was even the point of telling him?

"His, too?" A visible shadow veiled him. "He was in the war, you know."

"Noah wasn't in the war, Daddy," I said, thinking perhaps he thought that was the way he died.

"No, George."

My mother gasped. "Henry!"

"These are Noah's and my things, Daddy," I said. "George was Mommy's friend who was shot."

"Not her friend. Her husband."

"You're her husband," I said.

He nodded. "Yup. Son of a bitch."

My mother cupped my father's face in her palms. "You need a shave," she said. He pulled her close to him and clumsily kissed her cheek. My mother's eyes filled with tears. "Remember when we used to walk on the beach in the snow, Henry? Maybe we'll give it a try this afternoon. What do you say? For old times' sake."

He nodded, although neither of us were certain he understood—or even remembered.

She walked me to the door. "I'm sorry if I was harsh with you before. I'm tired."

"You weren't harsh." I hugged her. "Daddy knew what he was saying."

She nodded. "Certain things stay," she said sadly. "This is why he stays here with me."

I drove over the bridge from the Cape to the Mainland. My father always said there was no reason to drive over that bridge. That everything anyone could ever want was right there on the Cape. It seemed that everything I could possibly have wanted was right in front of me. For twenty-five years, I had searched for something in other places which only prevented me from feeling at home. Maybe my father was right when he said that you don't need to cross a bridge to travel great distances. Maybe you really just have to look into your soul and have a willing and brave heart. I wanted to be whole again. I was so weary of living in fragments. I was no longer satisfied with making love in the dark, or having conversations replete with omissions. I wanted to reclaim the person I once was. I was having a hard time remembering her, but I was certain that my mother was right. She was in there somewhere. Just like George was still in my father's memory. Somewhere.

CHAPTER TWENTY-EIGHT

Carl

Laura was no longer the skinny, scared little girl I met that night in Seaside. She was a beautiful woman with smooth mocha skin, perfectly arched brows, and dark hair pulled back straight from her forehead. She wore a slim gray pant suit and white V-necked shirt, accented by a string of pearls. And a glistening diamond wedding band.

"You look wonderful," I said.

"So do you." She turned to Mama. "Why didn't you tell me he was coming?"

"I had no idea," Mama said innocently.

I couldn't take my eyes off Laura. She was yet another piece of the puzzle I needed for its completion.

"How long have you been here?" she asked me.

"Since last Friday."

"So, you knew he was here when I called on Wednesday." She wagged her finger at Mama. "What am I going to do with you, Mary Lou?"

"Why don't you two get some coffee?" Mama asked, looking at her wristwatch. "Time for my nap anyway."

"Laura?" I asked.

"We'll be back in a bit," she said and leaned down to kiss my mother. "And I forgive you for not saying anything."

Mama smiled. "Take your time. You got a lot of catching up to do."

Laura and I were self-conscious as we rode alone in the elevator, staring as the numbers blinked down from five. I motioned her through the doors before me. She stopped to pull on her coat and I took it, holding it open behind her.

"My husband should take some lessons from you," she said, laughing. She had a hard time finding the arm of the coat and fumbled. "See? I'm not used to this."

"I'm on best behavior," I said, embarrassed.

"I see." She fastening a kerchief around her head. "Now, where should we go?"

"There's a place back toward Warrensville—Ernie's?"

"Oh, Essie's . . . Think it's cocktail time yet?" she asked with a laugh.

"Feels like it," I said as we walked outside. "My car or yours? I have a Blazer. Four-wheel drive."

"You win. Mine's just an airport rental."

"I didn't think flights were landing this morning."

"We got in yesterday morning," she said. "My husband is lecturing in Raleigh on Monday so we thought we'd make a weekend of it and then I could see Mary Lou."

"Where is he now?"

"At the hotel. He's not one for girl talk, though he's very fond of Mary Lou."

We drove the road in silence, our eyes fixed ahead as the wipers struggled to wash away the salt spray from the highway. Power lines lay under heavy ice here and there, and trucks with flashing yellow lights and cherry pickers were making repairs.

"At least the storm's passed through," I said.

She nodded. "So, where do you live now? Your mother wouldn't tell. I've know nothing about you all these years except that you're well. That's all she would say." She paused. "Even to me."

"She reads too many mysteries," I said, trying to make light of my mother's withholding.

Laura's voice became serious. "She was protecting you."

"She always did."

We pulled into the parking lot for Essie's. There were only a half dozen cars but the restaurant was open despite the fact that the power was out. Each table was lit by a single candle. We took a table tucked away in a corner even though the place was empty. I ordered a Jack; Laura had merlot. They brought us a platter of nacho chips and salsa, a cheese and fruit plate on the house.

"Well, this is a feast," she said, breaking off a chip. "So, you never answered me. Where do you live now?"

I nodded. "You go first."

"Why?" she asked, curiously tilting her head to the side.

I shrugged. "I suppose I'm more inclined to listen right now rather than talk."

"Well, let's see. I'm married to Benjamin Court for twenty-six years. Two daughters, Emma and Jolie, twenty and nineteen. We live in Chapel Hill. I'm a pediatrician, Ben is a pediatric neurologist." She hesitated. "That's a start. Your turn. Like it or not."

"Married to Olivia Hughes for twenty-two years. Two kids. Sophie's twenty. Daniel's nineteen."

"Guess we were on the baby track at the same time," she said softly. "Where do you live?"

"Willow, Massachusetts. We both teach at Belvedere College. Olivia teaches drama. I'm chairman of the department of physics."

"Physics? Why, I never would have thought . . ."

I shook my head with resignation. "Everyone reacts that way. But I like what I do," I said defensively.

"I thought you'd be another Billy Joel by now," she said. "What about the piano? The singing?"

I began the well-rehearsed speech that sounded like a closing argument. "There's a tremendous application of physics in music, you know. Sound waves and vibration. Take the piano, for instance. . . ."

"Joe, it's me," she said, reaching across the table and taking my hand. "You can't fool me."

I hung down my head. "I wasn't trying to. I left everything." I could feel tears welling in my eyes. Goddamn it, I thought. "See, nothing could be the same after I left, so I made it all different." I looked up at her. "My name is Carl Larkin now."

Her mouth flew open. "Wasn't he the teacher? What was it he taught?"

"American Literature. He died just before I left."

"I remember you telling me about him," she said thoughtfully. "Why his name?"

"I was seventeen. He was a good guy. Like a father to me. Something like that I suppose." Her hand still held mine and I tightened mine around hers. "I never got to say good-bye to you that night."

"Your mother called in the morning."

"So she told you what happened."

"She did." She paused. "She said how he shoved her and then she got up all her strength and shoved him into that wall and the way his head hit, it killed him. She said for sure the police would never believe it was her since, well, you know, since you and I . . . so she made you leave. She said there was no way on Earth they weren't going to hold you responsible. I told you back then we were just trouble waiting to happen. I warned you."

"That wasn't exactly what happened. She wasn't the one acting in self-defense." My heart pounds. "He would have killed her. Or me."

"Ssh. I know what really happened."

"What are you saying?"

"I knew she wasn't telling the truth all along. She couldn't. She would have compromised both of us that way."

"How did you know?"

"Because I knew you." She swallowed hard and spoke almost inaudibly. "Because there had to be an even better reason for you to leave without saying good-bye."

"Sometimes I think I was a coward not to have stayed."

"Oh, God, no. Not a couple months after you left, my mother sent me to live with my Aunt Flo in Chapel Hill. About a year later, she sold our house and came there as well." A sadness came over her. "We both crossed the line, Joe."

"How do you mean?"

"I told you, even back then ... that invisible line wasn't so invisible."

"I know."

"My mother and I were tormented." She took a long sip of her wine. "My mother was raped."

"Oh, Jesus. Who?"

"One of Clive Jenkin's posse. Bart Wilson."

"I knew him. He was one of Luther's drinking buddies. Scum. He was scum."

"Worse."

"I suppose he walked."

She shook her head. "He was never even arrested. He came into the house one night while she was sleeping, but it was his word against hers and hers was worth nothing. He left town for a while, until the heat died down. Every one of his cronies gave him the same alibi for that night. And everyone knew the truth but it didn't matter. My mother called Mary Lou the night it happened."

"My mother?"

"She trusted her. And she needed a white woman to help

her. Mary Lou took her to the hospital over in Raleigh and then she took her in for a few weeks while she healed. After that, Mom moved to Chapel Hill. She couldn't live in Warrensville after that."

"Mama never told me."

"Your mother is the most amazing woman I know, next to mine. She was afraid that if you found out, you'd come back home. And you would have, Joe. You can't deny that."

"I would have."

"You were like a vigilante in those days."

"Where's your mother now?"

"Still there. Rocking on the porch with my Aunt Flo. Two sweet old biddies." She smiled. "They live across town from us."

I reached for my wallet. "I have pictures."

She took them in her hand and smiled. "If I'd known you'd be here I'd have brought pictures, too." She looked up at me and down at the photographs again. "Now, Sophie looks like you and Daniel, he looks more like your wife."

"Daniel is too much like me."

"And you're oil and water," she said with conviction.

"How do you know?"

"Oh, because I know you." She handed back the photographs. "People don't change. You're like your mama. She's feisty and passionate and she'll defend what she believes is right no matter what the cost. Her heart is always in the right place and she doesn't fight unless she has to. You're not a bit like him. You believe that, don't you?"

"Sometimes I wonder. I was always in trouble."

"But never without just cause." She sighed. "And I didn't help matters. Didn't you hear what I just told you? Your heart was in the right place. Always. Luther didn't have one."

"What's Ben like?" I asked, wanting to change the subject.

"Wonderful. The only bad thing I can say about him is that

he's a slob and doesn't do things like help me on with my coat. And he works too hard." She looked apprehensive. "And Olivia?"

I looked at the picture as I tucked it back into my wallet and was filled with remorse.

"I never told her about me."

"She doesn't know what happened?"

"She doesn't even know my real name."

She shook her head in disbelief. "But she's your wife."

"I never knew where to begin and every time I started, it just seemed, I don't know, too risky. I was afraid of what she might think of me."

"You just begin at the beginning, Joe," she said tenderly. "My mother always said that was the best place to start."

"So did mine." I took a drink of Jack. "You think that's a southern thing?"

We laughed and I realized we were holding hands again across the table.

"What would you do if Ben told you something like that after all your years together?"

She thought for a moment. "Honestly? I'm not sure."

"Have you told him about us?"

"I have."

"And?"

"And we all have pasts. He's got his skeletons."

"Oh, so now I'm a skeleton."

"That's not what I meant." She looked embarrassed. "I've missed you, Joe."

"I've missed you, too."

"My dear, sweet Joe. I'm afraid you've missed far more than me."

My eyes filled with tears. "I'm heading home tonight."

"And you'll tell your wife the truth."

"I'm going to try."

"No. You can't just try. You have to."

Mama was awake when Laura and I got back to the facility. Neither of us believed she slept. It was all a ruse. Her hair was still combed and the bed was not in the least bit mussed, but neither of us said a word. It was nearly five o'clock. I needed to get back to Warrensville and check out of the hotel, which extended me the extra hours because of the storm. I promised Olivia I'd be back today and that was already a broken promise. If I drove straight through, I still wouldn't be back much before dawn.

"I'm coming back at Christmas, Mama," I said. I didn't want to leave her in the worst way. I wrote down my phone number and address and put it on the bureau. I made another copy for Laura.

"Before Christmas Day or after?" Mama asked.

"I'm not certain. I'll let you know."

Mama asked for a pen and paper and wrote down the name and phone number of the complex where she lives in Warrensville and also the Martins'. "You'll bring Olivia and my grandchildren next time, now, won't you?"

"I will," I said, although I was filled with uncertainty.

"And you call when you get back to Willow."

"Yes, I will," I said almost obediently. "And I'm going to take it nice and slow. You don't worry about a thing. No more fast cars for this boy."

I kneeled down by her chair. We were both crying. I kissed her cheek and it felt like velvet, just the way I always thought it felt. I refused to say good-bye. "See you soon," I said. "I love you, Mama."

Laura walked me to the elevator, which came too quickly. We embraced. "I'll look after her," she said. Her eyes brimmed with tears. "I'm going to stay a while longer. I won't leave her until I know she's fine."

"Thank you."

"You're welcome, Joe Parker," she said, squeezing me to her.

There was nothing between us anymore. But for me, she was someone who knew me once and found me again—and through it all, she told me I was the same.

I was lost in thought as I drove back to Warrensville. I gathered my belongings, paid my bill, and got on the highway. The pines were bent low from the weight of the ice. They formed an arch across the road and I imagined it looked like the kind of road that led to Heaven.

I was leaving home.

I was going home.

CHAPTER TWENTY-NINE

Olivia

Carl called from the road around ten o'clock on Saturday night. He apologized for being late, explaining that there were several last-minute things that needed tending. I knew better than to press him for the smallest detail. His answer would only have been evasive. I had decided to trust him and remain patient. But he sounded different to me. He said he was tired, yet there was an urgency in his voice. I couldn't decide whether it was anticipation, apprehension, or that he sounded beleaguered.

"Have you eaten anything? You're not driving on caffeine, I hope. "

"I'm OK. How about you?" he asked.

"I went out to Chatham earlier. My mother made barley soup."

"Margaret's famous snow-day soup."

I was relieved to hear what sounded like a smile in his voice. "It wouldn't be a snowstorm without it. I should have brought some home for you."

"It doesn't have the same effect if you're not in Chatham," he said. "Lots of ice there?"

"Some. We had the endless summer and now it's the endless winter."

"Be careful," he said.

"Careful?"

"On the ice. You're always rushing around."

"I am?"

"You don't think you scurry around? Watch yourself sometimes."

"Dad used to call me a whirling dervish," I said, laughing. "I don't even know what that is."

"A spirit who puts someone in a trance."

"How do you know that?"

"Ah, I know many things," he said, purposely mysterious.

"When will you be home?"

"As soon as I can," he said.

We hung up the phone and it occurred to me that it wasn't my father who had called me a whirling dervish, it was Noah.

🌀

I carried the boxes to the basement and, with sheer adrenaline force, the trunk as well, sort of sliding it on a blanket down the steps. I placed the windmill on my nightstand.

I let out Emmet and watched the snow flurry around the porch lights in a thousand directions. We have antiquated storm windows that gape at the sides and are relatively ineffective, and the wind came right through the walls and floors. Every year, we vow to replace them but then the spring would come and we'd put in the screens and forget how cold the winter had been. I swept up the ashes from the night before, placed a new log and fresh kindling in the fireplace, and gathered pillows and an old down comforter from the closet. I put Mozart's Piano Concerto No. 23 on the stereo and took a stack of magazines that I hadn't yet read, and Emmet and I waited.

🌀

I was in such a deep sleep that I never heard Carl's key in the door, but Emmet began to howl and took off with the energy he had as a pup. I heard footsteps heading for the stairs and a moment later Emmet came flying through the living room with another howl, pulling at my quilt and then running back into the hall, and coming back with Carl.

I leaned up on my elbow. "Hi."

Carl crouched down beside me. "Hey," he said, studying my face as if I was someone he barely knew and couldn't place. "What are you doing *here*?"

"What time is it?" I asked sleepily.

"Four."

"In the morning?"

"In the morning," he said gently. "So, how come you're not in bed?"

"Too cold up there."

He smelled like sweat and coffee and, at first I couldn't place it, whiskey.

"Have you been drinking?" I asked.

He laughed. "No, have you?"

"You smell like whiskey."

"Had a little Jack earlier."

I raised my eyebrows. "Oh, right. Your new best friend?"

"Hardly," he said.

We were awkward with one another. I started to get up from under the quilt, thinking I should go and comb my hair or something. He'd been gone a week and I must have looked a mess. Besides, the fire had died hours before and it was just as cold in the living room now as upstairs.

"Stay," he said.

"You talking to me or Emmet?"

"Both of you," he said as he placed more kindling and another log in the fireplace. He took off his shoes and pulled his sweater over his head and tossed it in the corner.

"Move over," he said and crawled under the quilt next to me, curling his body around mine.

☙

The living room faces east. I hadn't closed the blinds the night before and the morning sun streamed in around eight o'clock.

"So bright in here," he murmured as we awakened, still entwined around each other.

I nodded, certain he would close the blinds. Instead, he rolled on top of me. "I missed you," he said. "Very much."

I missed you, too, I thought. I was frightened without you. The thought of not having you here, not seeing you again, living without you.

He waited for my answer and then he kissed the side of my face, my neck, and my mouth. "Did you miss me, too, Livi?"

"I did," I whispered. "I did."

"Then tell me," he said.

"I missed you."

And then we made love while the sun bathed the room in gold.

CHAPTER THIRTY

Olivia

It doesn't take long for children to see that there is no such thing as a perfect world. Disappointment comes early on, if you think about it. Beginning with a broken toy, a fall from a bicycle, not making the team. You get older and seize what you know are glimmers of perfection—like when you first fall in love and you and your lover are the nucleus and the imperfect world revolves around the perfection of the two of you.

The last time my world was momentarily flawless was when Daniel was born. The time before that was when Sophie was born. That Sunday morning when Carl and I made love in sunlight, it seemed like forever since I'd felt that ideal sense of peace. In the sunlight, we were new lovers and yet there was a comfort that only comes with years of history and sharing a life. Whatever awkwardness we had felt when Carl first came home had melted away. We lay on the quilt side by side, our hands clasped together between us.

He stretched his arms over his head. "I need coffee."

"I'll come with you," I said.

"Look at this," he said as we walked into the kitchen. "What did you do?"

"Painted."

"More than painted," he said, running his hand along the wainscoting. "This is great."

I smiled and took the bag of coffee from the freezer. "I told you I was painting last night but you were too drunk to remember."

"I remember now," he said sheepishly, pushing back the hair from his forehead.

"I'm glad you like it. I wasn't sure." I looked around the room. "Pretty bold for me. Quite a departure from white, huh?"

He took the coffee from my hand. "You make it too weak."

"After all this time? How come you never told me before?"

We drank our coffee and then Carl carried his suitcase upstairs and we showered and changed.

"Well, I feel human again," he said.

Carl lit a new fire, adding three logs this time. I stood behind him, watching as he deftly broke kindling and placed it beneath the logs.

"That's going to burn all day," I said.

"So?"

"What if we want to go somewhere?"

"We won't," he said definitely.

"We won't?"

"Nope. Too cold. Besides, I've done enough driving to last me awhile." He put the fire screen back in place and stood facing me. "So, where do we begin, Livi?"

"We?" I asked softly. "Why we?"

"Because I can't do this alone." He took my hand. "Sit here," he said, pulling one of our wing chairs next to the fire. He took the other and placed it facing mine. He breathed deeply and his eyes filled with tears.

"I've got a lot to tell you."

"Oh, God," I said. I always think the worst.

He studied my face expectantly. "It's nothing bad, Livi. Just a real long story," he said.

My heart pounded. "Something's wrong."

"Something was," he said. "Jesus, I don't know how to be-

gin." He looked straight at me. "Now, my mother always said
to begin at the beginning."

I couldn't remember the last time he'd mentioned his mother.
Maybe the night we first met. "Go ahead."

"You're beautiful," he said.

I laughed. "Now you're really scaring me. Not to mention
changing the subject."

"No, you are beautiful. And I love you, Livi. As I tell you
what I'm about to tell you, promise me you'll remember that."
He leaned over and took my hands in his. "There was never a
fire."

"What?" Truly, I didn't know what he meant.

"My house didn't burn when I was seventeen."

I felt my eyes grow wide. "Then why . . ."

"I'm not from Matthew's Hill. I'm from a town about twenty
miles east called Warrensville. My name is not really Carl Larkin. My real name is Joe Parker."

I gasped and jumped from my chair. I was all right with a
different town but a different name was something else entirely.
"What are you saying?" I could barely catch my breath. "This is
insane."

"Just hear me out," he said, reaching his hand out to me. "I
prayed all the way back here that you'd understand."

"Carl Larkin doesn't pray," I said robotically, standing stiffly
in front of him.

"No, but Joe Parker once did."

I thought I was going to be sick.

"Livi," he said, coming over and kneeling in front of me.
"It's going to be OK."

"Are you in trouble? Did you do something, I don't know,
bad?"

"No," he said, holding up his chin. "I'm going to show you
something. Wait here."

He walked into his den and came back with the St. Christopher medal in his hand and the sneakers in the other. "My mother gave me this the night I left Warrensville," he said, letting the pendant dangle from the chain. "St. Christopher is the patron saint of travelers. Her name's inscribed on the back. See? Mary Lou."

I felt ashamed that I had already unearthed the pendant. "You said her name was Deirdre."

"It's Mary Lou," he said softly. "She's the reason I went back home."

"She's alive? How could you . . ."

"Listen to me," he said. "I know you have a million questions and I know they're all going through your head right now but you've got to just hear me out. Except for the night I left Warrensville, this is the hardest thing I've ever had to do in my life. Can you do this for me?"

I nodded.

"And I promise you, I will answer each and every question you have, and then some."

He kept the sneakers because he wore them the night he ran. When he spoke about Luther—he never referred to him as his father—he was twisting his hands so furiously I thought they might bleed. I pictured them wiping the blood from his mother's mouth. When he recounted taking off in the middle of the night, his eyes looked wild, much the same way I imagined they looked when he was a frightened seventeen-year-old boy who drove the darkened highway alone. I thought of Daniel, so tender and still wild at nineteen and shuddered to think how Mary Lou felt when she sent her son and only child into the night to save him, her medallion around his neck—the only way she had to protect him.

When he told me he'd had drinks with Laura, I wasn't jealous of her because he loved her once as much as I was jealous of the truths she knew about him. She knew he played piano and sang with the choir. I felt she knew my husband in more of a totality than I did. Carl made a point of reassuring me all the while he spoke of her, telling me about her husband and her children, and yet part of me knew that marriage wasn't necessarily a barrier against old lovers—whether they were dead or alive. Briefly, I wondered how I would feel if Noah appeared before me: Would I forsake Carl and the children or was this my life now? I pushed the thought out of my head. I had a twisted habit of provoking myself sometimes, presenting myself with unrealistic scenarios.

Carl finished, sat back, his fingers steepled on his chest, his head down. "That's it."

Carl had always held himself stiffly. That night, he sat in the wing chair, his shoulders relaxed, his burden visibly lifted. It would be false to say there was no sense of dislocation, of life displaced as it was reinvented, of submission.

"I'm afraid," I said.

"Of me?"

I shook my head. "I don't know," I whispered. My body was motionless. "Why didn't you tell me before? Because you didn't trust me?"

"See? I told you. You answer your own questions."

"Maybe because you always answer my questions with more questions."

"Maybe it's because until now I didn't have answers to my own. Or ones that I felt safe enough to share."

Sometimes there is a flight-or-fight persona that comes over me. I was numb. "We should have some supper."

He rose from the chair and held my shoulders. "Livi! Don't do this. Don't pass this off and say let's have supper. I didn't just tell you that I cracked up the car or got fired."

I began to sob.

"I didn't want to make you cry. Never. Not ever," he said, wrapping me in his arms. "I kept wanting to tell you and as time went on, I felt I'd lose you."

Despite his arms around me, I no longer felt safe with Carl. His dependable pragmatism, his reliable routines and emotional armor that once shielded me had vanished. He was suddenly a reflection of myself, as vulnerable as I with the now-revealed, tangible evidence that loss was something neither of us could overcome easily.

We had spent the last twenty years or so stumbling around in the darkness, calculating our conversations, careful to omit what might be painful or true, not realizing that omissions are as significant as confessions, if not more so.

But I wrapped my arms around Carl as well, needing him and feeling he needed me just as much. The room darkened slightly as clouds rolled over the sun and snow began to fall again. Plump slow flakes melted as they hit the ground, as though each begged for absolution.

CHAPTER THIRTY-ONE

Olivia

Carl shoveled the driveway while I made supper. Omelettes with peppers and onions and tomatoes and whatever else I could find that hadn't spoiled over the last week. I called my mother and Nina to say that Carl was home, assuring them that he was fine and we'd talk the next day. Nina was skeptical, insisting that something in my voice didn't sound quite right. My mother said something rather odd. "He's a good man, Livi," she said. "There's more to him than meets the eye. I'm sure of it."

Daniel called. I'd told Carl when he called the night before that I was forced to tell Daniel that Carl was in Warrensville. At first, Carl asked why I couldn't have made some other excuse, but I reminded him of Daniel's persistence, not to mention his ability to see through the smallest lies.

"So, is he back?" Daniel asked as I answered the phone.

"He is. Would you like to speak to him?"

"I guess," Daniel said.

"Hang on," I said and covered the mouthpiece, calling to Carl. "It's Daniel."

I stayed on the extension.

"Hey, how'd it go?" Daniel asked, an edge to his voice despite the tough attempt to be casual.

"Good," Carl said. "Really well."

"That's it? Good? You're gone for a week and that's all you have to say?"

Normally, Carl would have withdrawn, stumbling around for words or even taking an offensive. "No, that's not all, "Carl said. "But it's more than a phone conversation."

"How much more?" Daniel asked provocatively.

Carl remained undaunted. "You and I are going to have a long talk when you get home," Carl said.

"Oh, this is about me? You were the one . . ."

"Daniel," Carl said his name firmly. "No, it's not about you. What I'm saying is that I'm going to tell you everything, face to face."

I sensed Daniel's embarrassment. "Well, fine," he said. "I want to speak to Mom."

"I'm still here, Daniel," I said, silent until then.

"I knew you were," Daniel said.

Daniel acts like he always knows everything.

"Everything's fine," I said, trying to soothe my son. "I'll call you tomorrow. How's the snow there?"

"All right, I guess."

"I'll speak to you tomorrow, Daniel. I love you."

"Dad?" he asked. "You still there?"

Carl answered.

"Take it easy, OK, Dad?" Daniel's sixth sense kicking in, picking up on my cues that his father deserved a pass on this one. I breathed a sigh of relief, heartened that we would get through this.

෧

Carl and I set the coffee table in the living room and ate tatami style by the fire since the rest of the house was so cold. He brought in the bottle of wine I'd bought the day before.

"Pinot noir with eggs?" I asked.

"I would say that just about now, the last thing we have to

worry about is the marriage between food and wine," he said, pulling the cork from the bottle. "Don't you think?"

At first, we ate silently, shyly, the way two people might who are together for the first time.

"I went to Chatham last weekend," I said.

"You told me."

"Oh, right." So much had happened I'd forgotten. "And yesterday, too."

"Yesterday?"

"Just for a few hours."

"Homesick?"

I shrugged. "That's where I go when I'm upset."

"How was Henry?"

"Bad. Then good. Then bad. You don't know what to expect from one moment to the next. One minute he asks about his mother and the next he'll say something that makes him seem like he's his old self. It's like he's playing a cruel joke on us. "

"It's synapse," he said. "You see every momentary neurological erosion with dementia."

"That's so clinical. He's my father."

He looked at me, his fork suspended midair. "I'm sorry. Habit. How's your mother?"

"You know my mother was married once before," I blurted out. "When she was eighteen. He was killed in the war."

"She told you this *yesterday*?"

"Last weekend."

"What made her tell you?"

"Maybe it's something in the air. Confession week," I said bitterly. "People waiting upwards of twenty years to tell me the truth."

"Livi."

I ignored what appeared to be his protest. "So, we were up in the attic and I went through my old things, too."

"I didn't know you had old things there."

"Yeah. Things from Noah and me," I said, trying to be casual although as I said Noah's name aloud to Carl, I felt my heart skip a beat. "Honestly? I didn't want to. It was Mommy's idea."

He nodded. "And?" He smiled.

"Why are you smiling?"

"Because you call her Mommy."

"So?"

"So, it's sweet. I call my mother Mama." He hesitated. "So, what was there?"

"Well, first she showed me George's picture. That was his name. Her first husband."

"That must have been strange."

"A little. He was handsome. Not as rugged as my father, though. She was pregnant when she got the news that he was killed and then she lost their baby." I took a sip of wine. "My father knew him, too. He was friends with his older brother."

"Did she say why she hadn't told you before?"

"I seem to be a victim of bad-timing syndrome," I said sarcastically. "I feel like I've been hit over the head now. Twice."

"What else?"

"Nothing else," I said as I stood to clear the table.

"Don't do this, Livi."

"Don't do what? I'm clearing the table."

"You need to talk to me. Obviously, you went through your past, too. You said you found things from you and Noah."

I was suddenly angry. "Since when do you know what my needs are? Just because you went away and had some, I don't know, some epiphany doesn't make you some sort of expert when it comes to purging the soul! Maybe I don't feel like talking right now."

I never yelled at Carl.

Carl leaned back on his elbows. "Believe me, I'm no expert. And I'm not trying to force you."

"Good. Because you can't."

Carl gathered our wineglasses and followed me into the kitchen. I did the few dishes and washed out the fry pan while he wiped down the counters.

"Now what?" he asked, drying the dishes as I set them in the drainer.

"Nothing."

"I want you to be part of me, Livi."

"How can I be part of you when I'm not sure who you are? And what are you planning to tell the kids? Have you thought about them?"

"The truth," he said. "I'm going to tell them the truth."

"When? Twenty years from now?"

He ignored my remark. "When it's right," he said, walking away from me. "I'm going upstairs. I never unpacked my bag."

Not minutes later he was back, Noah's windmill in his hand. "What is this?" he asked.

"Where did you get that?"

"It was on your nightstand. Is it from the attic?"

"Just give it to me," I said, reaching for it.

"Where's it from? Did you make it?"

"Noah made it. A long time ago."

"And everything's in the basement except for this. Why?"

"It's not important."

Carl handed me the windmill and looked at me with an intensity I'd never seen in his eyes before. "Apparently, it is important. It's your turn now, Livi. You can't stand there and tell me you have no secrets. You can't tell me that in some ways you're not as culpable as I've been when it comes to omission."

"I told you about Noah. He was never a secret." I couldn't look Carl in the eyes.

"I've never really had all of you, have I?" he asked.

"That's ridiculous," I said. "How can you even say that?"

"Because you never talk about him."

"He's dead."

"That has nothing to do with it."

"I can't believe you're accusing me of keeping something from *you* after—"

"I'm not accusing you of anything. "

"You are! What is it you want? Am I obligated now to tell you that I loved him? OK, I loved him. That's obvious. I married him."

"And you were still married to him when you married me, weren't you?"

"I don't know what you're talking about. If you're trying to justify yourself, this isn't going to work." I shut the kitchen light. "I'm going to bed."

He took my arm and stopped me from walking away. "OK, but just tell me why he made you a windmill."

I stared at him. "It doesn't matter."

"You know, in physics, one of the first things we learn is about energy and the wind," he said. "Except it's a tough measurement to predict."

"I'm sure it's all very scientific."

"Noah was an actor though. I'm sure his interest in windmills had nothing to do with measurements and vectors, did it?"

"Why does this matter?" I demanded. "It really doesn't concern you."

He let go of my arm. "I suppose it doesn't. I'm sorry."

Carl went to the living room. Emmet followed him. I heard him toss another log into the fire. And then I heard the piano. I tiptoed to the hallway and listened. He played single keys at first, note by note, and then his left hand joined his right. He played "River" by Joni Mitchell, his fingers searching for the right notes as he went along, making lots of mistakes. He sang, softly, barely audibly but right on key. *I wish I had a river I could skate away on. I wish I had a river so long I could teach my feet to fly. Oh I wish I had a river I could skate away on. I made my baby cry.*

I let him finish. He hadn't seen me standing there.

"That was beautiful," I said. "And shocking."

"I told you that I used to play. My fingers barely find the keys anymore."

I stood beside him, the windmill in my hand. "He made this for me the night before our wedding. He loved the Navajos. They believed that the wind was the power within all of us. Noah said that together he and I would harness the wind." Tears ran down my face. "And then he died. So I guess he was wrong."

He rose from the piano bench and stood before me. He didn't push me to say any more. I still wasn't ready and somehow he knew and accepted that.

"But while you were together, maybe he was right," he said gently.

"Why didn't you pull the blinds when we made love this morning?" I asked in a whisper.

He didn't answer at first. He took me in his arms. "Because I don't want any more darkness," he said.

Our world didn't so much shatter as it transformed. There was an affirmation of what once only took place between us in the darkness and finally came to light. We were a duet, though the harmony was strained. The man who was my husband was not the man I thought he was. I had waited a week for Carl to come home. I wasn't quite prepared for the emergence of Joe Parker. He was at once a stranger and someone I knew but hadn't seen in a very long time. And so was I. In some ways, that was the harder part.

CHAPTER THIRTY-TWO

Carl

Olivia was shocked, and, of course, I knew she would be. She was overcome, sympathetic, angry, frightened. She ran a gamut of emotions that came in unpredictable crescendos over the next several days.

When I found the windmill, I thought it was something either she or one of our children made when they were small. But as soon as I held it up to her and saw the look on her face, I knew it carried a different meaning. I don't believe for a second that she left it on the nightstand carelessly. I think she left it for me to see, although she may not have been aware of that herself.

I knew she loved him but I never quite knew how. There were times, if I force myself to be completely honest and look back, when I felt Noah's presence between us. I suppose I opted to look the other way, guilty as I was that I had a secret life of my own. Revelations on her behalf would have required my own unveiling. How strange though that once she married a man who promised to harness the wind and then a man who measured it.

That night, I got into bed first, pillows propped behind my head, waiting for her. She came from the bathroom, her hair fluffed and her face pink from scrubbing. Maybe it was my imagination, but I swear she started to say my name and stopped. It is an indescribable feeling when your wife doesn't know your name. I was Carl to Olivia and had she called me Joe it would have felt so odd. Besides, I had been Carl for forty-one years. Funny, in Warrensville I was Joe and it felt right.

We didn't make love that night, although we slept laced together.

On Monday morning, we were exhausted. Any conversation over breakfast would have been unsatisfying since there was still so much more to say. We had to get to work, fulfill our obligations, yet there was an unspoken understanding that whatever more there was to say would have to wait. As always, I left before Olivia that morning, but, unlike all the other mornings for the past twenty-two years, I kissed her mouth and emphatically said, "See you later."

I brushed the snow off my windshield and did the same for Olivia's Jeep, backed down the driveway, and headed to Belvedere. Ginny was at her desk when I came in, wearing her trademark gray skirt, white blouse, and navy cardigan, her dark hair tied at the nape of her neck with a filmy chiffon scarf, engrossed in a page where she was filling in blanks. The sameness of her presence stabilized me.

"Morning," I said, trying to avoid too grand an entrance.

"Professor Larkin!" she exclaimed, rising from her chair. "Well, you look well."

"A week off will do that," I said casually, taking the weekend mail from her desk.

She followed me. "I haven't opened that yet," she said.

"It's OK," I said, sifting through the pile. I looked up at her. "How've you been?"

"Fine," she said haltingly. "Thank you. Professor, don't you want me to sort that for you first?"

I set the mail aside and slapped my palms on the desk. "So, what's new here?"

"Well, you were gone all week. . . ."

"Was I?" I teased.

Ginny blushed.

"May I see my appointment book, please?"

"*You* want to see it?"

"Please."

She brought it to me, dutifully, incredulously. "Anything else?"

"Coffee would be great," I said, opening the book. "I see I have a meeting with Professor Levin on Thursday. He's that young man up for tenure, right?"

"Right," she said, not taking her eyes from me, clearly amazed that I knew anything that was going on in my life, or that I wanted to.

"You have it scheduled for four."

"Yes?"

"Call him back and tell him we'll meet for lunch instead. Twelve-thirty if it fits his schedule."

"Yes, sir." She brought my coffee. "Anything else?"

"Nothing, thanks," I said. "Oh, you know what? Maybe later today you'll give me a lesson on the computer. I think it's about time I learned to use e-mail, don't you?"

ॐ

Ginny came back into my office around noon, a pad and pencil in her hand. "What can I get you for lunch today?" she asked.

"I'll grab something out," I said, taking my jacket from the coat tree. Poor Ginny. She was in abject shock.

I knew that Olivia had a break between one and two so I walked over to the Performing Arts building and waited for her in the lobby.

"Hey," I said as she came down the stairs.

"Hi."

"Want to get some lunch?"

She shook her head.

"Not eating today or just not with me?"

She didn't answer. As I said before, she was up and down.

"Are you angry or scared, Livi? Because both are acceptable, you know, and you can be both."

She looked to me the way she did when I first danced with her, when Noah's wedding ring tangled in the button of my shirt and she told me she was a widow. Vulnerable, I suppose, is the word I'm searching for.

She started to walk away from me, then stopped and turned around. "Both. Angry. Scared."

"Look, I didn't think for one moment that I'd come back home and unload a lifetime and you'd say something like 'Oh, that explains it' and life would just go on as usual. But you need to talk to me."

She looked at her watch. "We'll have to talk about this another time."

I looked around rather furtively, aware that students were walking to classes and our voices were raised. "Do you think we could discuss this now? Can't we find someplace more private?"

Olivia was obstinate. "I don't want to."

Truly, I was weary. "Do you know what it was like to fall asleep every night burying the truth and waking up every morning knowing it wasn't fully interred?" My voice was hushed but laced with frustration.

"Yes," she said softly.

"Well, then not talking to me isn't going to solve anything."

She looked away from me.

"This isn't doing either one of us any good, now, is it?" I asked, trying to stay calm. "I don't want to fight with you."

"We never fight. We've never fought," she said.

I smiled. "Well, then, maybe this is a good thing."

"Maybe."

Concession, I thought, taking her hand. "Come with me. Please."

"It's almost one-thirty," she said. "I have to be back at two."

"What's at two?"

"*Antigone* rehearsal."

"Get the TA to do it."

"What? I can't do that."

"Why not?"

"Because I can't."

"Come on."

"Have you lost your mind?" She took a step backward.

"I couldn't possibly be that lucky."

We walked to my car. I used her cell phone and called Ginny.

"Do I have anything scheduled for this afternoon?" I asked.

"Nothing, Professor," she said.

"How about tomorrow?"

"You're monitoring a TA's class."

"Oh, right. Cancel it."

"*Cancel* it?"

"Well, reschedule it. Make it Wednesday or Thursday or whenever." I thought for a moment. "Ginny, how do you feel about dogs?"

"I love dogs," she said.

"Great. Listen, my house keys are in my top left desk drawer. Can you take care of Emmet for, I don't know, until tomorrow?"

"Emmet?"

"Our dog. He's a big guy with a loud bark, but he's an old softie. Just let him out tonight and in the morning and leave a light on for him. Oh, and food and water. The food's in the mud room off the kitchen."

Olivia listened to the conversation with her mouth open. I covered the phone. "You're going to catch flies," I said.

At that point, nothing was going to shock Ginny about my new behavior patterns, although Olivia was still having a hard time with them. Besides, for Ginny, taking care of Emmet must have made her feel needed. I told her we'd be back by Tuesday night.

"How do you hang this thing up?" I asked, turning to Olivia. She was staring at me. "Is there a problem?"

"What are you *doing*?" Olivia asked.

"Running away with my wife," I said.

"Where are we going?" She almost smiled.

"Nowhere," I said.

We drove to Vermont, Mad River Valley, about three hours from Willow, and found an inn.

"Tell me you've been here before," Olivia said as we pulled up the drive.

"Only under an assumed name."

"Not funny."

"I thought we could use some levity."

"Seriously, how do you know about this place?"

"I don't," I said, parking the car. "Serendipity."

"I'm hungry."

"Well, let's see what's what," I said.

We checked into the inn and the clerk said that about a half mile down the road there was a restaurant. He gave me the room key and asked if we had luggage. We'll have some lunch first, I said, and be back.

"He probably thinks we're having an affair," Olivia said as we walked back to the car.

"With any luck, maybe we will," I said, hugging her to me.

The restaurant was in a small white clapboard house. Tables were set for dinner with white cloths and blue dishes. "We're not dressed for this at all," Olivia whispered as we waited for the host.

"Two," I said as the maître d' approached us.

"We don't open until six," he said.

"Do you have a bar? Can we get some drinks and a basket of bread?"

"It'll be about an hour until we serve though, sir."

I looked at Olivia, who nodded.

We ordered a bottle of wine.

"I have nothing with me," Olivia said.

"What do you mean?"

"I have no toothbrush. No comb."

I laughed. "Well, I tell you what. I'll buy you a toothbrush and a comb. Under the circumstances, it's the least I can do." I raised my glass to hers. "Truce?"

"Truce," she said, clinking her glass to mine.

"Now, you have a choice. You can tell me why you're scared and why you're angry."

"That's not a choice."

"Well, you get to choose the order."

She laughed.

"So, which one first?"

"I'm scared because I'm angry and I'm angry because I'm scared." She looked at me and her eyes filled with tears. "Does that make any sense?"

"Perfect sense."

She took a deep breath. "My mother made me go through Noah's things," she said. "I hadn't looked at them since he died."

"Why did she do that?"

"Because she said the heart has enough room for everyone and I needed to . . ."

I waited for her to finish her sentence.

"Let go," she said.

"Of him?"

"Yes."

"Did you believe her?"

"Not at first."

"Now?"

"Yes."

It reminded me of the first time we met and I fired questions at her to keep the conversation going.

"And?"

"But I don't know who you are now," she said. "I don't even know what to call you."

I hung down my head. "I am who I always was," I said. "And I've been Carl Larkin for the better part of my life. And I mean better, Livi. The better part of my life has been with you. And the kids."

"But I didn't know so much of you."

"That's not true," I argued. "I kept things from you. I kept parts of myself from you. But I didn't change. I didn't pretend with you." I sighed.

"But that's not true. You play piano. You sing. You have a mother who's alive. An old girlfriend. . . ."

I interrupted her. "Livi, you have to give me a chance."

"But the parts you kept, what if . . ."

"What if you don't like them? "

"That's not what I was going to say."

"Yes, it was. Be honest."

"I am. I don't know what I was going to say. I don't know what to think."

"Let me ask you something. Are you guiltless? Can you sit there and tell me that there aren't parts of you that you've kept back? It took you twenty-five years to go through the attic. Do you mean to tell me that there weren't things you left unsaid even until last night? Until just moments ago? And that there still isn't more to say?"

"But I didn't pretend to be someone else."

"Maybe I had no choice. Maybe I'm like no one now. Not Carl. Not Joe." I looked up at her. "It's like with your father."

"What do you mean?"

"He's not Henry. He's this stranger to everyone around him. Maybe even to himself."

She reached across the table and took my hand. "Is that how you feel?"

"Yes."

"Am I making you feel that way?"

I shook my head. "No, but don't shut me out. And I know that's asking a lot because I shut you out."

"I loved Noah very much. When I lost him, I lost everything. When I met you, I felt like I betrayed him." She raised her eyes to me. "And then when you were gone, I missed you." Her voice broke. "And then you came back and it wasn't you."

"Maybe it was just the rest of me," I said.

"I mean, what do I do with all this?"

"What do you want to do?"

"There you go again," she said, smiling.

We stopped after dinner, before we went back to the inn, and bought toothbrushes and a comb at Olivia's insistence. When she wasn't looking, I bought a dozen candles. She came from the shower that night before bed and I'd lit them all. She crawled into bed, naked beside me.

"Pretty," she said. "And very sneaky. When did you do all this?"

"You took a long time to choose a toothbrush."

She laughed. "Actually, it was the comb that threw me."

I ran my hand along her thigh. "I love you, Livi," I said, pulling her closer to me.

"I love you, too," she said. And she looked right into my eyes.

"So, now we know. This is what we do."

CHAPTER THIRTY-THREE

Olivia

In the ten days that preceded Thanksgiving, it seemed that Carl and I never stopped talking. There were no more startling revelations or unearthed secrets, just changes. They were seemingly imperceptible but, at the same time, took our breath away.

One afternoon we went to the basement and I showed him the trunk. We were down there for hours. And with the details of my life revealed, he remembered more of his.

The day before Thanksgiving, we picked up Sophie at the train in Springfield, dropped her at home, and went back to Bradlee Airport for Daniel. We had agreed that we would tell the kids about their father when they were home and could look into his eyes. And first we wanted to get through Thanksgiving.

"You're *both* here?" Daniel asked as he came through the gate.

Daniel definitely needs to be in some sort of law enforcement when he grows up. True, usually I was the one to pick him up at the airport, figuring it would avoid conflict between him and his father, but he was overly suspicious when he saw us together. "What's going on? Grandma and Grandpa are OK, right?"

Carl put his arm around him as we walked to the car. "Everyone's fine."

"So, then . . ."

"Why am I here, too?" Carl asked.

Daniel nodded.

"Why not?"

And I thought he was the same old Carl, answering questions with questions.

I was late getting to Chatham. As always, Carl and Frank would come up Thanksgiving morning with the kids. By the time I arrived, Nina and my mother had cooked nearly everything but the pies. They were sitting at the kitchen table, a bottle of wine and a plate with a wedge of cheese and crackers between them.

"What's that?" I asked.

"Camembert," Nina said.

"Ah, haven't had that in years."

"What's wrong?"

"Nothing," I said taking a slice, waiting for a roll of thunder or a bolt of lightning.

"What's with you?" Nina asked.

"Do I have really obvious body language?"

"In general or this moment? And, yes, you do."

"Where's Daddy?" I asked.

"On the sun porch. Watching the Sound," Nina said.

How do you watch the Sound, I thought. Such a paradoxical thing to do. He watches the Sound, he hears the sea, I mused, playing with words in my head. I took a glass of wine and went to the porch. He was in his rocker, looking out the window.

"Daddy?" I said. "What's going out there?" I could have sworn he'd aged since I last saw him two weeks before.

He searched my face, clearly not recognizing me.

"It's me. Livi."

"All right," he said, his head bobbing up and down, almost catatonic.

I sat beside him, afraid to take his hand, thinking he might feel threatened somehow. We watched the Sound together and then I went back to the kitchen, leaving him to stare silently at the moonless night.

I poured another glass of wine and started the pie crusts with Nina and my mother. "He didn't know me," I said to no one particular.

"He gets worse toward evening," my mother said. "You got here at a bad time. He's just tired." She was trying to comfort me as well as herself. "You'll see, by morning he'll be himself again."

"What's himself?" I mumbled. I'm not certain if she heard.

"Have you had dinner? We had a late lunch–early supper around four-thirty," my mother said. "There's spaghetti in the fridge. Some salad."

"Not hungry," I said, rolling out the crust.

Nina came up behind me and put her head on the space between my shoulder blades. "He wasn't bad at lunch," she said. "He even told a war story, right, Mommy?"

My mother laughed. "Oh yes. It was slightly convoluted and much in need of translation, but he tried."

I smiled. "Was he the hero?"

"He always is," my mother said.

Nina and I stayed up after our parents went to bed, putting the finishing touches on the table. Nina brought four bouquets of flowers, yellow spray roses, baby's breath, and sprigs of what looked like tiny blue cornflowers. Normally, we took my mother's low vase and made an arrangement, placing it beside the cornucopia centered on the table. We decided to do something different and took nine votive jars that my mother kept in the cabinet in case of hurricanes and made an individual bouquet for each setting. We cut the flowers down low, sitting at the kitchen table, fitting them into the jars. I found a tiny American flag stuck on a toothpick in the cutlery drawer.

"Hey, look at this," I said and placed it in my father's bouquet. "You think he'll notice?"

"He'll salute," Nina said. "Livi, how's Carl? You haven't really told me anything."

"Good."

She raised her eyebrows. "So, what was it all about?"

We hadn't told anyone. Not yet. "It was about . . ."

"You don't have to tell me," Nina said.

"I will tell you. One day."

"Are the two of you OK?"

A smile crossed my face.

"Well, that answers my question," she said, putting the last of the votive bouquets on the table. "There. Now, I say we go to our spot and have a nightcap. You game?"

"Tea and amaretto?" my mother asked, appearing in the doorway.

"You're supposed to be sleeping."

"This is what happens in old age. When you're young, you have babies and all you do is want to sleep and they don't let you. Then they're teenagers and you wait up for them until all hours, and then they move out, and just when you think you'll finally get some sleep, you can't."

"Maybe you should stop drinking tea and just go for the amaretto," Nina said.

"Such a fresh girl," my mother said.

And then the three of us took our seats by the beveled window and drank our tea while the beacon flashed on and off in the distance.

"I don't think I've sat here in years," my mother said dreamily. "We should do this more often." She turned to me. "You're brand new, aren't you, Livi?"

"What do you mean?"

"You know what I mean," she said. "I was right, wasn't I?"

"Yes," I said, laughing. "Once again, you were right."

✿

Carl and the kids arrived early the next morning, each carrying a shopping bag.

"What's all that?" I asked.

Daniel grinned. "Dad went crazy last night."

"Completely nuts," Sophie said. "And why it's my ovarian function to clean up after him and your son is beyond me." She gave Daniel a playful shove.

" 'Cause you do it so beautifully and with great style," Daniel said.

"Ugh. Don't even talk to me!" Sophie said.

I peeked into the bags. There were three deep dishes wrapped in foil. "It sure smells good."

"Have a look," Carl said, beaming. He lifted out bowls and set them on the counter. "Wait, where're your folks and Nina?"

My mother and Nina came in.

"Wait, I want to get Henry, too," he said.

Carl came back with my father walking beside him in shuffling steps. "OK, Henry, here we go," Carl said, unveiling the delicacies with all of us standing around. "Now, here we have candied yams with bourbon. Southern style. Real Kentucky bourbon, corn syrup."

I couldn't believe it. This was a man who never boiled water.

"You want to do the honors?" Carl asked Daniel, shoving a foil-covered baking dish in front of him.

Daniel peeled back the foil. "I helped with these. High-rise biscuits."

"Made with cream of tartar and half-and-half and plenty of butter. Not for those watching their diets," Carl said.

"He *baked*?" I whispered in Sophie's ear. "Was it a mess?"

She rolled her eyes. "You don't want to know."

"And the pièce de résistance," Carl said, lifting a glass lid off a deep dish. "Southern cornbread and oyster dressing."

"Oyster dressing?" my father piped in. "Where in hell did you get oysters?"

"Fish market, Henry," Carl said. He took a spoon from the drawer and scooped out a bit, holding it to my father's mouth. "Taste."

We waited until my father swallowed.

"So, what do you think, Henry?" Carl asked.

My father nodded appreciably.

"Well, now, that's the vote that wins the prize," my mother said.

Nina looked at the clock. "I wonder where Frank and Jillian are," she said.

"There's probably traffic," I said.

Just then the door opened and Frank and Jillian came in. Frank opened a bottle of champagne and we all toasted Thanksgiving and counted our blessings. My father lifted his glass and cried "Here's to the red, white, and blue" and began to sing "My Country 'Tis of Thee" off key and mixing up the words.

Daniel came up to me. "Dad's gone crazy. I'm telling you. I think he crossed the Mason–Dixon line and came into the Twilight Zone."

"What did he do down there?" Sophie asked. "You said you'd tell us when we were all together."

"Later," I said.

"Can't you just give us a clue?" Sophie begged.

"Basically, he just went home," I said.

"I think he's possessed," Daniel said.

And I thought that it was quite the opposite. Carl had finally rid himself of his demons. And I'd acknowledged mine.

EPILOGUE

Chatham—Almost One Year Later

Olivia

We told Sophie and Daniel the truth, as promised, the day after Thanksgiving last year. We were back in Willow, the four of us sitting around the fireplace, having leftovers.

Carl and I had gone over the ways to tell them dozens of times in the last few weeks. We thought of not telling them until the summer when we'd have them home for a longer period of time, and then decided that was just postponing the inevitable. We braced ourselves for their anger and confusion.

It was far easier for Carl to tell the children than it was to tell me. He started by saying "Mom knows," and although they listened to each word as Carl spoke, they both looked at my face with silent pleas asking for approval. A few times, I nodded nearly imperceptibly, reassuring them that their father was a man who needed both understanding and forgiveness.

Carl's tone was even and confident. He conceded both his grief and regrets, yet insisted there was a time and place for everything and that this story couldn't have been told any sooner. The kids were more shocked to discover they had a grandmother in Warrensville than they were to learn that their brutal grandfather had perished at their father's hands. There was never any doubt in their minds that Carl not only acted in self-defense but to protect his mother as well.

It was Sophie who asked if Carl would have gone to Warrensville if Robbie hadn't shown up in his office that afternoon. And Carl said he would have, eventually, but Robbie's appearance was good fortune because he might have gone back too late, if not for that. Daniel cried while Carl spoke. His tears surprised me more than they surprised Carl. My tough boy, whose muscles ripple on his arms and pulse in his neck, is much like my husband. In some ways, he's like my father as well. Parts of them fear their own sentiment. Daniel wiped his cheeks with the back of his hand, and when Carl rose from his chair to comfort him, Daniel laid his head on Carl's shoulder. It was Daniel who said that Robbie was in some way Carl's destiny.

"You believe in destiny?" I asked.

"Do you?" Daniel asked, and Carl and I laughed as Daniel answered with a question the way Carl does.

"Well, I do," I said. "And I think it's something that can't be changed or manipulated. Things happen for whatever crazy reasons."

When Carl finished, I gathered the dishes and Sophie followed me into the kitchen.

"It would have been worse if you weren't there, Mom," she said. "You validate it all."

"How's that?" I asked.

"You know, it's like, if it's OK with Mom, then it's OK. It's always been that way." She put her arms around my waist as I stood at the sink and leaned her head against my back.

"My mother still validates things for me," I said.

"Like what?"

I turned around and smiled. "Everything."

"I hope I'm like that with my kids, too," she said.

"You will be. From what Daddy says, I think Mary Lou is like that with him as well. You have a strong legacy, Sophie."

"I'm going to go sit with Daniel and Daddy, OK?" she said, kissing my cheek.

I did the dishes and thought about my mother. If she wasn't at my father's side, his illness would appear far worse. Even now, as my father has worsened, it is undoubtedly her perseverance and spirit that allows Nina and me to love him and not just his specter. It's because of my mother, even when he rants and raves, that we seize the lucid moments and savor any glimmer of memories, even if they appear to be vagaries filled with inaccuracies. It was my mother whom I will always credit with forcing me to the attic that day. It was her sanction, her affirmation that a broken heart can mend, that loving again doesn't mean you've forgotten or negated what once was.

Later that night, after we spoke to the kids, I came down to the kitchen for a glass of water. Sophie and Daniel sat at the table, picking over the last of the turkey and oyster dressing. Daniel had a bottle of beer in front of him. He jumped when I walked in, the bottle nearly toppling.

"You're not driving anywhere, right?" I asked calmly.

"I can drive on more than one beer," he boasted, puffing out his chest the slightest bit.

"Well, that's good to know. A great talent."

Sophie shook her head at Daniel. "Big shot," she said. "You can be such a jerk."

"Not such a big shot," I said, and kissed the side of his head. "But it's nice to see that everything's more or less normal. And you better never drink and drive."

"I don't," he said earnestly. "I was showing off."

"No kidding?" I said.

Of course, life was better than normal. It was real.

Their questions came days later and lasted for weeks. Even now, a full year later, they still ask questions. And Carl gives them answers. Between Christmas and New Year's last year, we all went to Warrensville and visited Mary Lou. We flew into Raleigh and rented a car. Carl stopped along the way to show us the house where he lived, the beach at Seaside, an old juke joint that's now a restaurant. He took us past his high school and out to River Road where the falls tumble furiously into Thunder River. He didn't take us to the cemetery. We agreed it would have been far too devastating for the children to see Carl Larkin's grave, and surely there was no reason to see Luther's.

Mary Lou is adamant that her assisted-living facility is called just that. The word nursing home is anathema to her. She is a beautiful woman, true to every way that Carl described her. I was nervous about meeting her, wondering if I would hold up to Laura, with whom she remains so close. Carl spoke to the woman at the desk.

"We're here to see Mary Lou Parker," he said. "She's expecting us."

"And what is your name?"

"Joe," he said easily. "I'm her son. My wife Olivia and the grandchildren."

To her, he would always be Joe.

He knocked and called through her door. "Mama? We're here."

Hearing my husband's voice calling his mother made me weak in the knees. She opened the door, one hand covering her mouth, her eyes brimming with tears.

Carl has his mother's eyes, although they're not as blue. He has her languid movements, her sweetness, and the fire in her soul. It amazed me that my husband was able to reduce himself to embers for forty years.

Carl took her hand and introduced us one by one, and as he did, she hugged and kissed us as if she'd known us for a lifetime.

We spent four days in Warrensville. She had photo albums and a box of memories, from Carl's first shoes to detention slips (something that thrilled Daniel no end) to an old cassette of Carl playing piano at the preacher's house that we listened to on her old tape machine.

The photographs were of Carl as a young man, a boy, not much younger than Daniel. There was one taken in summer, shirtless, his arm around Mary Lou at some sort of fair. His stomach was taut and his hair was long and wavy.

"Where was this taken?" I asked.

"At the carnival," Mary Lou said. "There was a time when the carnival came to town every June. They had an antique Ferris wheel and the best cotton candy you ever could want." She turned to Carl. "You remember, don't you, Joe?"

"I'll never forget," he said.

We left on New Year's Eve day. I took bunches of photographs, promising to make copies and return them.

"When are you all coming back?" Mary Lou asked before we even said good-bye.

Carl looked at me. "In a month or so."

I took her hand. "Never mind the 'or so.' And maybe you'll visit us in the spring? We'll come to get you."

"I'd like that," she said. She took my hands in hers. "If I'd known all those years he was with you, I might not have fretted as much." She looked at her son. "You take good care of her."

"He does," I said. "He always did."

❧

It is early April and still cold in Massachusetts. The crocuses are poking through the earth. My father always said that's a sure sign of spring. In a few weeks, Carl and I will go to Warrensville and bring back Mary Lou. Just for a week, or as long as she wants to stay.

There is no doubt in my mind that a man who loves his mother the way Carl loves Mary Lou is a good man. My husband has a strength and certainty, a sense of who he is, despite the years he spent running. I believe it's because she loved him so well.

Today is Sunday and we are in Chatham. We did convince my mother, finally, to have someone come in to help with my father during the week. Her name is Caroline Brady, and for some reason he insists upon calling her Brady. She's a strapping woman who listens raptly to his now-only-occasional war stories and manages to distract him well enough to eat and bathe and cooperate. When he doesn't cooperate, Brady is nonplussed, and when he sleeps, she brings my mother tea and makes certain that she rests, as well. But Carl and I've been driving up here every Sunday for the last few months, except for the weekends when we've gone to see Mary Lou. Sometimes we come to Chatham on Saturday night and stay over. We are peaceful here and, this way, my mother doesn't have to be alone. We told Mommy and Frank and Nina and Jillian Carl's story not long after we told the children. As for our few friends and colleagues, there was no need to tell. Carl is Carl to all of us, and Joe to Mary Lou, and although it sounds like it might get confusing, it really doesn't. We've learned that names have little to do with identity. As for who we are, I suppose no one really knows us as well as we need to know ourselves—and one another.

In the last year, I have told Carl about the rooftop garden, the mural behind the bed, the Monday night ritual at Jefferson Market, and that I kissed Noah on the gurney as they wheeled him through the emergency room doors. But I never told him the details that belonged to Noah and me—those things that were intimacies of our life together. Carl is my husband: Those are not secrets I keep from him—they are merely memories from another life. Those are the ones I store in the corner of my heart. And I never asked Carl how it felt to see Laura again. Carl is allowed his corners as well.

I am sitting on the sun porch now, in my spot below the beveled window. My mother is in the kitchen, tending to a roast, baking popovers, watching The Weather Channel. It takes her places she knows she'll never go—California, Europe, Asia, the Middle East. Today she is visiting the Matterhorn. She is not unlike Mary Lou, who travels through her books.

I look out across Nantucket Sound and see the lighthouse in the distance and my father and Carl with Emmet on the pier. My father is bundled in a down jacket. A wool hat pulled down over his ears. Carl wears a plaid shirt and navy fleece that I bought him last Christmas. He stands behind my father holding a fishing rod, my father's hand on top of his. They bring their arms back in unison and toss back the line. They must have done this a hundred times in the last half hour.

It is hard to believe that once I sat in this very spot and mourned, convinced my life was over. Daniel and Sophie have still not asked about Noah. My past, unlike their father's, is nonexistent. I am—as my mother is to me—the glue, as Carl calls it. Even when my mother told me about George, it was hard to picture her as anyone other than a woman who had always been my mother.

It is inevitable that one day, in some way or another, someone will break Sophie's and Daniel's hearts. I pray they will not suffer what Carl and I endured separately, and then overcame together. I hope whatever pain they have is brief and heals quickly. When the time is right, I will tell them about Noah and explain that life is filled with detours that lead to possibilities and, sometimes, even miracles. Carl and the children are *my* miracles. I will tell my children about the chambers of the heart and its ability to heal and store memories and old loves. I only hope I tell them as convincingly as my mother told me.

The weather suddenly changes. This is common for the Cape. I watch as Carl and my father come toward the house, their steps fighting the pull of the damp sand. Their heads are bent down as they trudge forward, bracing themselves against the wind. Emmet lopes ahead, snapping at the blowing sand. Carl lifts his head as they near the house and waves to me in the window. I hear them come through the door. I hear my mother's voice and I know she is taking off my father's jacket and brushing the sand from his shoes. I listen to them as she coaxes and he argues like a child, and I think in two more weeks it will be Thanksgiving again and my parents are both still here.

Carl comes to the sun porch and kisses me. His lips are cool against mine. He sits beside me and puts his arm around me. I lean my head on his chest as we gaze over the Sound. I think back to that stormy day in Boston when we met and marvel at what the wind blew in. We are enveloped in each other.

We know who we are. We are at peace.

About the Author

Stephanie Gertler is the author of three novels: *Jimmy's Girl*, *The Puzzle Bark Tree*, and, most recently, *Drifting*, all published by Dutton. She also writes a lifestyle column for two Connecticut newspapers, *The Advocate* and *Greenwich Time*. She lives with her family and four dogs in New York.